Marrying The Boss's Daughter

Wintersoft's CEO is on a husband hunt for his daughter. Trouble is Emily has uncovered his scheme. But can she marry off the eligible executives before Dad sets his crazy plan in motion?

* * *

"I may be a gentleman, but I am not sleeping on the floor," Brett declared.

Sunny eyed the large, imposing bed, and a tremor of uncertainty scuttled up her spine. "Why is it that everything around you seems to be linked to royalty?"

Brett frowned. "What?"

"The bed. Is it a king or a queen?"

The corner of his mouth started to lift. God, she hated it when he did that. It was so sexy.

"Isn't there a phrase for it?" she persisted. "Something about being careful who you make your bed with, or who you're crawling into bed with?"

"Me," he stated firmly, his smile disappearing. "You're crawling into bed with me." The statement was bald, decisive and unadorned. Then he tempered it. "For a king's ransom. Free room and board."

Sunny took a deep breath. "I agreed to help you…but I never imagined this."

Dear Reader,

Egad! This month we're up to our eyeballs in royal romances!

In *Fill-In Fiancée* (#1694) by DeAnna Talcott, a British lord pretends marriage to satisfy his parents. But will the hasty union last? Only time will tell, but matchmaker Emily Winters has her fingers crossed and so do we! This is the third title of Silhouette Romance's exclusive six-book series, MARRYING THE BOSS'S DAUGHTER.

In *The Princess & the Masked Man* (#1695), the second book of Valerie Parv's THE CARRAMER TRUST miniseries, a clever princess snares the affections of a mysterious single father. Look out for the final episode in this enchanting royal saga next month.

Be sure to make room on your reading list for at least one more royal. *To Wed a Sheik* (#1696) is the last title in Teresa Southwick's exciting DESERT BRIDES series. A jaded desert prince is no match for a beautiful American nurse in this tender and exotic romance.

But if all these royal romances have put you in the mood for a good old-fashioned American love story, look no further than *West Texas Bride* (#1697) by bestselling author Madeline Baker. It's the story of a city girl who turns a little bit country to win the heart of her brooding cowboy hero.

Enjoy!

Mavis C. Allen
Associate Senior Editor

Please address questions and book requests to:
Silhouette Reader Service
U.S.: 3010 Walden Ave., P.O. Box 1325, Buffalo, NY 14269
Canadian: P.O. Box 609, Fort Erie, Ont. L2A 5X3

Fill-In-Fiancée

DEANNA TALCOTT

Marrying
The Boss's
Daughter

SILHOUETTE *Romance*®

Published by Silhouette Books

America's Publisher of Contemporary Romance

Special thanks and acknowledgment are given to
DeAnna Talcott for her contribution to the
MARRYING THE BOSS'S DAUGHTER series.

With special thanks to Julie Barrett, Kim Nadelson and
Mary-Theresa Hussey. Your kind words and creative spirits
always steer me in the right direction.

 SILHOUETTE BOOKS

ISBN 0-373-19694-6

FILL-IN FIANCÉE

Copyright © 2003 by Harlequin Books S.A.

Visit Silhouette at www.eHarlequin.com

Printed in U.S.A.

Books by DeAnna Talcott

Silhouette Romance

DeANNA TALCOTT

grew up in rural Nebraska, where her love of reading was fostered in a one-room school. It was there she first dreamed of writing the kinds of books that would touch people's hearts. Her dream became a reality when *The Bachelor and the Bassinet,* a Silhouette Romance novel, won the National Readers' Choice Award for Best Traditional Romance. Since then, DeAnna has also earned the WISRWA's Readers' Choice Award and the Booksellers' Best Award for the Best Traditional Romance. All of her award-winning books have been Silhouette Romance titles!

DeAnna claims a retired husband, three children, two dogs and a matching pair of alley cats make her life in mid-Michigan particularly interesting. When not writing, or talking about writing, she scrounges flea markets to indulge #1 son's quest for vintage toys, relaxes at #2 son's Eastern Michigan football and baseball games, and insists, to her daughter, that two cats simply do not need to multiply!

FROM THE DESK OF EMILY WINTERS

~~Six~~ Four Bachelor Executives To Go

Bachelor #1: Love, Your Secret Admirer
Matthew Burke—Hmm...his sweet ~~assistant~~ clearly has googly eyes for her workaholic ~~boss~~. Maybe I can make some office ~~magic~~ happen.

Bachelor #2: Her Pregnant Agenda
Grant Lawson—The guy's a dead ~~ringer~~ for Pierce Brosnan—~~who wouldn't~~ want to fall into his strong, protective arms!

Bachelor #3: Fill-in Fiancée
Brett Hamilton—The playboy from England is really a British lord! Can I find him a princess...or has he found her already?

Bachelor #4: Santa Brought a Son
Reed Connors—The ambitious VP seems to have a heavy heart. Only his true love could have broken it. But where is she now?

Bachelor #5: Rules of Engagement
Nate Leeman—Definitely a lone wolf kind of guy. A bit hard around the edges, but I'll bet there's a tender, aching heart inside.

Bachelor #6: One Bachelor To Go
Jack Devon—The guy is so frustratingly elusive. Arrogant and implacable, too! He's going last on my matchmaking list until I can figure out what kind of woman a mystery man like him prefers....

Chapter One

"Phillip, if it's any consolation, you've always looked particularly good surrounded by a bevy of beautiful females," Brett Hamilton told his brother. He cradled the phone between his ear and shoulder, and pushed back from his desk. He'd been so happy to hear from his brother, yet this bit of news surprised him. *Another girl? Again?* "At least you know the baby's healthy," he said. "It's the luck of the draw whether it's a boy or a girl."

"It's Mother and Father that are the problem. They dote on the girls, truly. But they want a grandson, Brett. An heir. They figure I haven't been doing my job, and they're looking to you now."

Brett said nothing—he'd heard it often enough in the past few months. His entire family kept reminding him it was time to get married, to produce an heir, to strengthen family alliances. It was all a bunch of rubbish as far as he was concerned. Producing heirs to keep their titles and traditions was a thing of the past.

"By the way," Phillip added, "they've struck up with

Lady Harriet again, and Mother said she's asking about you.''

"Phillip, must you ruin a perfectly good day, bringing that up again?"

"Well, it's true. Anyway, you're both getting to the place where you should think about settling down."

"Perhaps. But not together."

"Our families do complement each other," Phillip reminded him.

"What you're really suggesting, Phillip, is one of the greatest financial mergers England has seen in decades. Between their family business and ours we'd have a corner on the market."

"And is there anything wrong with that?"

"A merger and a marriage are two different things."

"And what about getting an heir in the process? Mother and Father would be ecstatic. I tell you, with the doctor promising us another girl, me and my swarm of females don't offer the family lineage a lot of hope."

"Four daughters and a wife do not create a swarm. Unless," Brett chuckled, thinking of the chaos he'd witnessed last summer, "you are on an outing to the park. And as for the family lineage, I think we are in dire straits if the only concern is to produce a male heir. I'd like to think we've moved beyond that."

"Huh." His brother sighed audibly. "Not to hear Father. The first thing he asked when we told him the news was if it was a boy. And Mother? She went into a veritable depression for a week when she found out the doctor said we should start adding more pink to the wardrobe. Carolyn says this is absolutely the last baby…so, little brother, even though I have tried my best, truly, you are now responsible for the family title—or at least an heir for it." He paused for emphasis. "What with their upcoming visit, I'd imagine Mother and Father will take the opportunity to remind you of your duties and obligations."

Brett squeezed his eyes closed, grateful his brother

couldn't witness his exasperation. His parents had been nagging him for years to settle down and get married. "So you're warning me?"

"No. I'm telling you what to expect."

Brett said nothing, but the burden of it all hung like a dark cloud over his head. He'd been told since childhood to embrace his title, and he'd been well schooled in his responsibilities. It had been an unspoken understanding that he would marry and marry well. But for him, London had been a place of spectator events, charity balls and social finagling. He'd grown up as Lord Breton Hamilton, but inside he simply felt like "Brett."

When the opportunity to move to America to work in Wintersoft's Boston office as vice president of overseas sales came up, he'd jumped at it. In the past six months he'd led a useful, fulfilling life, and he loved the challenge—and the anonymity—of it. Perhaps the software company didn't have the tradition of his father's shipbuilding empire, but Brett was quite content to build his own dream, to create his own niche.

"Well?" Phillip prodded. "What about your love life? You've been suspiciously quiet about all of it since you moved to the other side of the ocean. It's made Mother think that maybe you've had regrets, and with Lady Harriet, perhaps that absence has made the heart grow fonder. She even mentioned that Lady Harriet might consider joining them on their visit to Boston. She hinted to Mother that she's never been there."

The suggestion pulled Brett out of his reverie and caused him to sit erect in the leather desk chair. "What?" A second slipped away as he tried to assimilate what his brother was telling him. "No. Absolutely not."

"Why not?"

"Well, for one thing, I'll not be forced into a marriage, and for another, we're simply not compatible. We established that two years ago."

"You grow to like your mate, Brett."

Mate? Damn, he loathed the functional term. The woman he'd spend the rest of his life with would meet his expectations on every level, including the emotional and the spiritual. The last thing he needed was Lady Harriet tagging along on his parents' visit. "But I've grown to like my girlfriend," he said coyly, thinking that if he said he already had a woman in his life, they'd drop the whole thing. "Here. In Boston."

"Say again?" Brett heard two sharp raps, most likely against the receiver. "I do say, there must be something wrong with the connection. You? Have a girlfriend?"

"More than that," Brett continued boldly. "We're engaged."

A moment of dead silence followed his declaration.

"I beg your pardon, man? And you've been keeping it quiet? What a cagey old bloke you are!"

"I'm not trying to be cagey." But Brett's enthusiasm for the broad picture he'd painted grew. If his brother believed the tale, maybe Brett could get off the hook with his parents, as well. He'd had quite enough of their hints—and their ultimatums. "And there's more," he claimed, baiting his brother with one last delectable tidbit that had soared through his imagination. "We're living together."

"What? And you've stayed mum about all this?"

"I wasn't quite prepared to tell everyone. Not yet."

"You realize you have just poked a hole in our parents' carefully laid plans?"

"Mmm. Maybe. But you can see that if Lady Harriet chose to surprise me with a visit—well, it would be most...uncomfortable."

"For who? Mother and Father? Or you?"

"You will let them on to this delicate—or indelicate—situation, won't you?" Brett suggested shrewdly. That was always the fun of it, getting Phillip to do his bidding and soften up his parents. Phillip, four years older, had always delighted in his baby brother's teasing ploys and had spent a lifetime covering for him.

This time, however, Brett would admit the truth to his brother *after* his parents were safely back home and Lady Harriet had moved on to happier hunting grounds. He hated to deceive Phillip, but there really was no help for it.

As he was ruminating his way around this particularly tricky scenario, Sunny Robbins rapped on the frame of his open door. Seeing he was on the phone, she politely held up a file folder of contracts he'd requested an hour ago. He motioned for her to come in.

Sunny, who had the most mesmerizing gait of any woman who walked through Wintersoft's legal department, crossed the threshold and entered his domain. She was wearing that same short skirt again. The one he'd noticed her in in the employees' lounge last week. Huh. Short enough to play with a man's imagination, long enough to be respectable.

She had coltish legs, and they matched her demeanor— a little unconventional and very unencumbered. He'd always wondered about her, and had recently struck up several conversations with her that stopped just short of him asking her out. She was the paralegal who worked for Grant Lawson, general counsel for the company.

"I've got the copies," she whispered, preparing to put them on his desk.

"Wait," he mouthed, lifting a finger and listening to his brother's tirade.

She slid them onto the corner of his desk and took a step back.

"I don't believe it! Someone has snared my little brother? The man who always said it would take one resourceful temptress to steal his bachelorhood? That was the most inviting thing about you and the girls, you know. You were unattainable."

At that precise moment, Sunny threaded her fingers through her tawny locks and raked the chin-length riot of blunt-cut, windswept hair back from her temple. Her smile, patient and unaffected as she waited for him to get off the phone, accelerated his heartbeat. Their gazes collided and in that brief pause he saw something in Sunny Robbins that he'd never before recognized—a vision that coincided with the remark Phillip had made about his "resourceful temptress."

"Yes, well, I'm one step closer to giving it up," Brett confirmed, determined to stick to the charade but equally uneasy about the direction his wild ploy was taking him.

"Who *is* this woman?" his brother pressed. "What does she do? Where is she?"

"Actually, she's right here," Brett declared recklessly. "Sunny," he said, "blow my brother a kiss, will you, luv?"

Sunny blinked and a frown popped onto her brow. "Excuse me?"

"Blow him a kiss. From your lovely lips to my only brother, half a world away."

"Why?" Sunny slanted him a dubious look.

Brett grew magnanimous, as he always did when he carried a plot too far. This one was going to get him in big trouble, he knew. He could just feel it. "Because he wants to meet you! Tell my brother I love my job, I love my life. Blow him a kiss and assure him all is well with the world. That all is well with you." He handed Sunny the phone.

She stared at it as if he'd taken complete leave of his senses. When she finally, reluctantly, accepted it, she put it to her ear and listened, as if she expected to hear something absurd.

Then, to Brett's delight, she made a sloppy smacking noise into the receiver.

"Yes, I'm fine," she said tentatively.

Brett's smile grew, and his confidence multiplied. He couldn't help it; he looked at the conference call button and popped it on.

"And I hear you're living with my brother."

"I'm what?" Sunny exclaimed, stiffening as she yanked the phone away from her ear.

Brett punched the button off, effectively silencing his brother, and quickly made a dive for the phone. ''She didn't want anyone to know. Not just yet,'' he hastily explained to Phillip.

''Sunny? What kind of name is Sunny?'' his brother pressed.

''Hers. Solely, uniquely hers.'' Brett shook his head and flapped a hand at Sunny. He didn't want her to run out the door without an explanation. ''I'll be done in a moment,'' he mouthed. ''Look, explain to Mother and Father about this, will you, Phillip?'' he said, raising his voice. ''I mean, they're going to find out anyway, and it would probably be best coming from you.''

Phillip chuckled. ''I expect I'll need to tell them to book a hotel, too. Under the circumstances.''

''Do that,'' Brett agreed.

They said their goodbyes, but Brett's gaze was fixed on Sunny the entire time. She was rooted to the spot, and her eyes were huge. There was barely any color in her face save for a spot of red staining each cheek. Her chin was raised at a defiant angle, and her shoulders straightened, stretching the sheer fabric of her blouse and making the tiny buttons between her breasts shift.

Uh-oh. He may have gotten away with it with his brother, but he wasn't going to get away with it with *her*.

Brett carefully placed the phone back on the hook and set his hand on the file folders. He tapped them impatiently. ''Thank you for dropping these off, Sunny—''

''It's my *job*,'' she emphasized.

''And about this other little thing... I'm in a bit of a fix.'' He waited for her reaction. There was none. ''So...since you were in here, I thought you could help me out.''

''Your brother said—if I heard him correctly—that we were living together?''

Brett rose up out of his chair slowly, so as not to alarm

Sunny. "Now, there's the thing. We could, actually. If you wanted to."

Sunny's curvaceous lips parted and her jaw slowly dropped.

Before she could protest, he quickly came around the desk and added, "My parents are pushing me to wed a woman I simply don't love, you see. A nice woman, a nice family, nice connections, nice everything. Too nice, too convenient and too unfeeling. I made up this story about my girlfriend in Boston—and then, when that worked, I embellished it. To the part where we're living together."

"Embellished?" she repeated.

"I had to. No other choice, really." He threw up his hands. "My parents are coming for a visit. And they're threatening to bring Lady Harriet."

"Oh, my." One of Sunny's exquisitely arched eyebrows rose slightly, as if she hadn't heard him correctly.

Brett sighed heavily and glanced at the open door. He moved toward it. "There are some things you don't know about me, Sunny." He quietly closed the door. "None of them bad," he assured her quickly. "Actually, I've had a great life, and my parents are good people. But they're not…average people."

Sunny's gaze narrowed suspiciously. "Say it, Mr. Hamilton."

"There. Right there. That's the thing. In England, my friends know me as—" he cleared his throat before continuing "—Lord Breton Hamilton, son of Lord Arthur and Lady Miriam Hamilton. I regret to say it, but my family is titled." He uttered the last four words as if they were an extraordinary burden.

Sunny didn't move a muscle, not one. There was not so much as a wiggle of her lips or a flicker of an eyelash. "So you're rich," she said finally.

He shrugged. "I won't be, not if I'm disinherited, as they threaten."

"But I don't understand what that has to do with me blowing your brother kisses, or why we're living together."

The way she said it gave him a glimmer of hope. She hadn't dashed cold water on all his outlandish plans. And those plans were just beginning to take shape—with her help.

"Sunny, sit down. Please." He pulled up an overstuffed chair for her, then sat in the one opposite it. "I'll try to explain it all, but it's complicated. And the truth is I'd rather just be me. Brett Hamilton. I haven't told anyone over here about my heritage because I don't really want anyone to know."

"You're asking me to keep your secret."

"If you would."

Sunny offered up a half laugh, as if the situation was beyond ludicrous. "I'm not going to go running up and down the halls, claiming to know that Brett Hamilton is an English lord. Who would believe me?"

"Thank you." He impulsively reached for her hand, but just as quickly reined himself in. It would not do to become familiar with Sunny, not under the circumstances. "Along with my title comes some responsibilities. My brother called because he's just learned that the doctor predicts they are having their fourth girl. It doesn't matter to my brother and his wife, but my parents really wanted an heir. A child to inherit and carry on the family name."

"Ah, one of those archaic, gender-oriented issues."

A jolt of pleasure rose in Brett. Maybe this woman shared his beliefs. "Exactly. They are pressuring me to marry—and they've pretty much selected my future wife. Lady Harriet. The woman has it all—the family, the title, the connections. It would be a match—but one without any *spark*. And I really want that in a relationship."

Brett noticed Sunny's eyes visibly soften. Apparently he'd said something that struck a nerve.

"I couldn't help myself," he continued. "I told my brother I had a girlfriend, and I then I made it worse by telling him that we lived together.'' Sunny rolled her eyes, her eyelids fluttering in disbelief. ''You came into the room, and I said your name without thinking. I didn't mean to. You were just there, and it happened. Look, the stage is set. Unthinkingly on my part, but set just the same. Would you consider pretending to be my girlfriend, just while my parents visit?''

Sunny hesitated. ''You want me to make nice with your parents for an evening or two.''

''Well…'' He lifted a persuasive shoulder. ''Maybe more than that. I told them we were engaged.''

She groaned. ''Oh, Mr. Hamilton.''

''Brett,'' he said quickly.

''You can't be serious.''

''I am.''

''This is ridiculous.''

''I know, luv. It is. But the calendar won't wait. They're coming next week. Just pose as my girlfriend. We'll say we're engaged, and you can move in and we'll make it look as if we're living together.''

Sunny stared at him. Then she yanked her short skirt down to just above her knees and held it there with the heel of her hand. ''Let me make this perfectly clear. I walked down the hall to drop off file folders, not move in with you.''

''Sunny, I've got a two-bedroom flat—I mean apartment. You'd have your own room. And while my parents are here, we'd have a grand time, I'd see to it. Granted, the idea is preposterous, but everything else would be above-board and innocent. I promise.''

Sunny looked at Brett and thought the man had lost his mind, but one phrase echoed in her head: two-bedroom apartment. Since her wandering, homeless parents had moved in with her, she was in a quandary. There wasn't enough room for all of them and she didn't have the heart to insist they find somewhere else to light. ''Let me get this straight. You have a two-bedroom apartment?'' she asked.

''I know it's small,'' Brett said apologetically. ''The three bedroom wasn't available.''

His response was so quick it had to be genuine. Brett had a reputation at Wintersoft of being easygoing and amicable. He typically looked like he didn't have a care in the world—but now he looked worried, almost trapped. That bothered her, even as she guessed at the monthly rent on his apartment. ''And this apartment of yours is located where?'' Sunny asked. ''Because if it's all the way on the other side of Boston—''

''At that big complex Lloyd always recommends to all his new employees. The Liberty Tree Apartments.''

A ripple went through Sunny. If her mother were here, she'd say it was a sign, that it was preordained and that forces in the universe were aligning themselves for a ''Sunny'' moment. ''That's...where I live,'' she mused.

Brett brightened. ''Then you could commute,'' he said hopefully. ''Your apartment to mine. At your earliest convenience, of course.''

''You mean I could just move into your place, like a roommate?''

''Of course.''

''I wouldn't ask, but I have family living with me now, and it's...crowded.''

''Sunny, I have plenty of room. You're welcome to it. Pose as my *engaged* roommate,'' he wheedled. ''I think we'd get on famously, or well enough for a couple of weeks, anyway. All you'd have to do is to dote on me and convince my parents we were meant to be together.''

''You make it sound so easy.''

''It won't be,'' he warned. ''My parents are being quite stubborn about this. They may not like you at all, but you'd be doing me a huge favor.''

Sunny could feel herself giving in. They *did* have something to offer each other, even though she had serious doubts about gazing into Brett Hamilton's eyes for the next few weeks. The man exuded sex appeal—and she had no intentions of falling victim to it. He also had a reputation as a playboy.

"Sunny? What can I do to make you believe me?" he said earnestly. "I don't want to be dishonest with my parents, but I am quite weary of being reminded I have a duty, one that includes marriage. I don't want my nuptials to be used as a bargaining tool in the boardroom, and I don't want to produce heirs merely to carry on the family name. I'd like to genuinely fall in love with the woman I choose to marry."

"That was quite a speech," she said, considering.

"It's how I feel." He reached over and covered her hand with his. "Really."

"Oh, Brett…" She unconsciously used his first name. "How can you put me in this position? I'm not sure this is right, and I may live to regret it, but—" she looked at the concern in his eyes, the drawn expression of his features "—okay, I'll do it."

He broke into a relieved smile, and Sunny knew immediately that while it might be the right decision to help him out, living with him was definitely going to wreak havoc with her senses.

"When do you want me to move in?" she asked cautiously.

"We really ought to get to know each other. Is tomorrow too soon?"

Chapter Two

Carmella Lopez, executive secretary to Lloyd Winters, CEO of Wintersoft, was cleaning off her desk when Brett Hamilton walked into her office, file in hand.

"Lloyd said he needed these. They're suggestions for the contract changes for the overseas markets."

Carmella took the file, thinking that Brett was one eligible bachelor who shouldn't be overlooked. "Fine. I'll see he gets them. He's in a meeting now, and I expect it to run late. But you? Duty calls. I'm not letting you out of here until you sign these." She pushed a stack of papers at him.

Brett grimaced and checked his watch. "Can they wait? I'm meeting someone and—"

Carmella drew back, surprised. "Brett? I've never known you to weasel out of anything that has to do with work."

He grinned. "I know. But I'm getting a new roommate. And I'm meeting her after work."

"Her?" A sudden, guilty flush crossed his face, making Carmella only more curious. "Okay, what gives?" she pressed. "Is there a lady in your life that we don't know about?"

"No." As if feigning indifference, he pulled the papers to his side of the desk.

"Brett, I know you. And you look guilty as sin," Carmella accused. "Out with it."

"It's nothing," he protested, his attention riveted to the required signature line. "Everything's innocent. But because it's someone who works here—"

"What?"

He sighed heavily. "What is the matter with me today? I'm making a habit of saying too much of the wrong thing. It's good I'm not in the sales department."

Carmella pinned him with her gaze. She wasn't going to let him off the hook.

"Well, I don't want anyone thinking office collusion, office romance or anything. You won't mention it to anyone else, will you?" When she made a cross over her breast. He paused momentarily, then sucked in a deep breath. "It's Sunny Robbins, from legal."

"No!" Carmella sat back in amazement. She'd had no idea that Sunny and Brett even talked—and now they were moving in together? This would put a new twist on Emily's plans to pair him off with Josie, in public relations.

Brett shrugged. "Sunny needed a place to stay and I needed someone to help me out when my parents visit next week. It made sense. And I—" he flipped to the last page for one more signature "—I don't want to keep the lady waiting."

"Tell me first. Exactly how is she helping you out with your parents?"

He moved on to the next paper, then signed with a flourish. "Sunny is going to move in with me and pose as my girlfriend," he said. "Of course, there's nothing to it. But my parents claim to have the ideal woman picked out for me—and I just want to show them I can pick my own friends. My own *girl*friends."

"My." Carmella's plump hand fluttered to her chest. "That's the kind of plan that'll get you into trouble."

"I don't think so. She's just going to fill in for me."

"Brett, you might be surprised. That girl is a sweetheart."

He looked up at her and grinned, pen poised over the next document.

"Guess I'll have to find out, won't I?"

Shaking her head in mock dismay, Carmella wagged her finger at him. "I suggest you take this seriously."

"Come along, luv. Sunny's only moving in for a couple of weeks and just for fun."

Emily, the only daughter of Lloyd Winters, and senior vice president of Global Sales, popped her head in the door. "Um, I'm not trying to eavesdrop, but..." she hesitated, frowning at Brett "...did I hear you say Sunny Robbins is moving in with you?"

"Not like *that*," he exclaimed, capping the pen and handing it back to Carmella. "Sunny has family at her place, and I needed a little feminine touch in mine, so we worked out a deal."

Emily's head swiveled, and Carmella knew just what she was thinking.

"You and Sunny. Really?"

He nodded. "Mutual benefits, that sort of thing. In fact—" he rolled his wrist over and checked his watch again "—I'm meeting her now. Provided she doesn't think I've stood her up. Look, Em, Sunny and I just don't want to get this all mixed up with work. So you won't say anything, will you?"

"Absolutely not! I only came in because Carmella buzzed me, not because I was keeping tabs on you."

"The thing is, it's all come about quite suddenly, and I'm in a fix—but I don't want to give anyone here at the office the wrong impression."

"She's also posing as his girlfriend," Carmella interjected.

"She's what?"

Brett shifted uncomfortably. "Emily, you've been a great friend to me, so I guess I can tell you that my parents seem to think they have the perfect woman picked out for me. I'm determined to show them I can find my own. I don't need their help."

"Oh…" A dawning realization lit Emily's features. "Well, I agree! You go, Brett. Go." She shooed him out the door. "Don't keep your new *roommate* waiting."

Brett buttoned the center button on his suitcoat, then lifted a hand. "Thanks."

"And Brett…?" Emily asked.

"Yes?"

"Have fun."

The moment Brett walked out the door, Carmella and Emily exchanged glances. Significant glances.

"Okay. What gives?" Emily asked.

Carmella lifted both shoulders. "A minute after I buzzed you to let you know Todd Baxter was here, Brett walked in."

"Wait," Emily interrupted, her gaze straying to her father's closed door. "Todd's here? In there?"

Carmella nodded, whispering, "Apparently, with all this downsizing, he lost his job."

"I heard about his job, but puh-leeze." Emily shot a second wary look at the door to her father's office. "I don't get it," she muttered. "Why does my dad always treat Todd like the son he never had?"

"Oh, honey. Don't think like that. Todd's just down on his luck right now. He wanted your dad's advice, that's all."

Emily lifted a shoulder noncommittally and finally said, "Funny, isn't it, that Brett's trying to avoid the same situation I got roped into?"

Carmella pinned Emily with a sympathetic look. "Mmm, I know. Parents mean well. Apparently Brett's parents have someone in mind for him—not unlike someone else we both know and love.''

Emily shook her head, and Carmella knew exactly what she was thinking.

Years ago, Lloyd Winters had hoped to marry Emily off to one of the executives at Wintersoft—and, remarkably, he'd managed it! To the former Wintersoft wonder boy now sitting behind door number one, Todd Baxter. But Emily had married Todd for all the wrong reasons, and the marriage immediately crumbled. They'd divorced less than a year after their wedding. When Todd left Wintersoft, Carmella knew it was because he'd finally realized his chance to take over the company as Lloyd's son-in-law ranked right on par with the status of his marriage certificate: null and void.

But Lloyd apparently still wasn't convinced that his daughter couldn't be happy with one of the successful bachelor executives at his company. The big-hearted widower thought he had his only child's best interests in mind, but Carmella knew that he wouldn't stop trying to match her up with someone until she was married. In fact, she'd heard him talking about it.

So Carmella had helped a desperate Emily hatch a plot to systematically marry off every bachelor in Wintersoft. It would take Emily off the hook and put her right where she wanted to be: single, free and unattached.

Brett was the next man on their hit list. When they'd discovered he was an English lord, they knew that they'd have their work cut out for them. They figured it would take a sophisticated, worldly woman—and they'd agreed Josie was all that and more. But now, after all their efforts, he'd just waltzed in and announced he was moving in with the wrong girl!

"You know, I feel kind of sorry for Brett," Emily said softly. "Been there, done that. But what about Josie? I was certain she'd be perfect for him."

"I don't know about Josie. But I think we should keep his secret."

"*Their* secret," Emily reminded her.

"Sunny, of all people," Carmella mused, picking up the documents Brett had signed. "Sunny and Brett... It's an odd combination. But then, they say opposites attract." She momentarily pondered Brett's signature. It was the same, but rushed, hurried. Not like him at all. "He says it's nothing, but I get the strangest sense from him. As if he's awfully eager to have Sunny as a roommate—and that makes me wonder. It really makes me wonder."

Sunny picked the most secluded corner booth in the Keystone Coffee Shop and waited for Brett to arrive. He wanted to talk to her privately after work, so they could hammer out the details of their new living arrangements.

She would never admit to him the real reason she was playing the part of the smitten fiancée. It wasn't so much to help him as it was to help herself. She needed to get away—and Brett had unwittingly provided her the opportunity. Her parents were driving her *crazy.*

Not in the same way Brett's were, of course.

No, since they'd moved in with her a month ago, they'd taken over—and Sunny felt helpless to stop it from happening.

Her parents had that way about them. They just *did* things. Aggravating things.

Now Sunny's windowsills had been taken over with little peat pots of scraggly herbs that flavored dinners of tofu stir-fry. Her bathroom, once decorated in lush shades of green, had become a jungle of hand-washed clothes because her mother didn't think laundry detergent was good for the environment. Worse, Sunny's thick, fluffy towels were now air dried—and wound up as stiff as cardboard and as scratchy as sandpaper.

And that wasn't the half of it.

She couldn't bear to recount her father's quirky habits and eccentric ideas.

Her parents claimed they were going to move out. As soon as they found something. But they were making noises about finding an acreage in Vermont. Of raising goats and tapping sugar maples. Of living off the land.

It was an idealistic dream—one they couldn't afford. And until they realized it, they'd be shacked up at Sunny's, making her perfectly reasonable life insane and chaotic.

That was the real motivation behind Sunny's agreement to help Brett: peace of mind. A little normalcy.

Living with an English lord might not be normal, but it was guaranteed to be proper and quiet and staid.

She'd settle for that. Gratefully.

In spite of the cool fall weather, Brett had shed his suit coat and strode into the coffee shop rolling up the sleeves of his tailored white dress shirt. Tall and darkly tanned, he *was* good-looking, Sunny grudgingly admitted. The kind of man who turned heads in his wake.

Brett's gait was confident, athletic. His long arms swung loosely at his sides, and his wide shoulders and lean belly did great things for his business attire. She could imagine him in dungarees and a cotton knit sweater, too, his sinewy arms working the ropes of a sailboat. Heck, if his family was some kind of royalty they probably had a yacht. Maybe he just stood at the helm of it, like a hood ornament—or whatever they called it on a boat—with his hands folded behind his back, looking regal and important.

It fit, all of it.

His hair, the color of sun-drenched sand, was full-bodied, and so textured it actually reminded Sunny of ripples on the beach. His eyes, aquamarine-blue, were darkly fringed and deep set—as if made for staring out across an endless ocean.

Yet it was his accent that had caught Sunny's attention all those months ago. Charming and bold, it added a musical, almost lyrical, quality to his deep, rich voice. The way he smiled when he talked made his mouth move sensuously, as if it had a will of its own.

All the women at Wintersoft rolled their eyes and fanned themselves in mock palpitations every time he walked by—and usually he'd toss off a teasing comment or a taunt. He was every bit the playboy who knew how to make feminine hearts flutter. Yet whenever Sunny stood next to him in the elevator, he barely nodded at her, or offered up some innocuous comment about the weather.

Their few encounters had left her feeling as dull and ordinary as the elevator music.

How, she asked herself, was she going to manage living with *him?* The Greek god of the English aristocracy.

He'd already predicted that his parents wouldn't like her. Heaven help her, what had she gotten herself into?

"Sunny," Brett acknowledged, slipping into the seat across from her. He leaned so close she got a whiff of his aftershave, a tangy scent of saltwater and surf, heat and sand. "Sorry I'm late, luv. Lloyd wanted those contracts, and Carmella had papers for me to sign."

"You know," Sunny said wryly, "Lloyd's daughter is the one you should be dangling in front of your family like a girlfriend."

"Emily?" He looked surprised. "But she's the boss's daughter. Of course, she is rich. I suppose my parents would like that."

"Well, I'm not rich," Sunny informed him. "And it doesn't look like I'm going to be. So please expect your parents to be highly disappointed."

He chuckled as if she had said something extraordinarily funny. "Money isn't everything," he said. "They'll appreciate your sensible qualities and your nice personality."

Sunny bit down hard on the inside of her lip. "That," she said, "is what people say about women they are trying to pawn off on a blind date." Her voice drifted into a falsetto as she repeated the age-old line: "'You'll like her, she has a real nice personality.'"

Brett's irresistible grin widened. "And cheery sense of humor," he added.

"I have a *common* sense of humor," she stressed. "Think common. As in *commoner*."

He waved it off, unaffected. "It doesn't matter, Sunny. Really. In spite of our differences, I have to believe my parents will come around. At least enough to let me out of this trap they insist on calling marriage."

Sunny stared at him, realizing he had no idea how great their differences were. "I would have thought," she said slowly, "that since you know so many of the women at the office, you might have asked one of them instead."

"I..." He looked confused and lifted a shoulder. "I don't really know any of them well."

"But I've often seen you talking to all sorts of women." Flirting, she wanted to say.

"Office demeanor," he dismissed. "You know how some people like to carry on."

Sunny was debating whether he was serious or not when the waitress, named Hazel, according to the plastic name tag pinned to her plump chest, stopped at their table. "Coffee?" she asked, simultaneously pulling a pencil from behind her ear and a notepad out of her apron pocket, "or something special?"

"Cappuccino," Sunny said.

"A pot of tea, please," Brett ordered. "With sugar and lemon."

The waitress slid him a disbelieving look. "You into that antioxidant stuff, sonny?"

Brett's lips twitched. "No, luv. That old English stuff," he answered, pumping up his accent and giving her a broad wink.

The waitress snorted. "Cute," she grumbled, jamming the pad into her pocket. "Everybody's got to be a comedian. And they all think I got the time for it."

As Hazel hurried away, Brett and Sunny looked at each other.

His eyes crinkled at the corners. "I don't think she believed me," Brett confided, his voice lowered.

Sunny felt the beginnings of a smile curve her lips. "Apparently not."

"She probably wouldn't have believed me if I professed to be an English lord, either."

"Probably not."

"That is a bit difficult, here in America, you know."

Given Brett's self-deprecating demeanor, some of the tension that had Sunny in knots subsided. She'd arrived at the coffee shop convinced Brett would lay out a list of expectations for her. He'd give her the dos and don'ts, all the while making her conscious of the haves and have nots. Instead, he'd come into the coffee shop with an apology for being late and a smile. Maybe she'd never given him a chance in the first place.

Brett sat back and openly studied her. "I don't know why we haven't really talked before," he said thoughtfully.

"I imagine because we're supposed to be working." She shrugged, knowing that wasn't the reason at all. He'd probably dismissed her as an underling. "You're busy. I'm busy."

"Mmm. Well, no matter. But I did want to talk to you about this—" Brett quickly glanced around to make sure he couldn't be overheard "—lord and lady thing. So it's probably good this came up as it did with the waitress. I would appreciate it if you would keep it in the strictest confidence. No one at the office knows."

"But why?" Sunny lifted both shoulders. "I'd think you'd want to have that little prefix in front of your name. It must come with its own set of perks."

"And responsibilities," he said dryly. "No, I'd much prefer to just be me."

Sunny didn't believe him. Not for a moment. Here was a man who had been born with a silver spoon in his mouth. He'd probably grown up in a castle, or on an estate that had been handed down through the generations. He'd most likely gone to private schools and worn jodhpurs instead of jeans when he went riding. "That can't be easy, Brett. Adjusting to life without your title?"

"What isn't easy is being different. Or being treated differently."

Brett, Sunny realized, apparently didn't have any idea how difficult being "different" could be. "Come on. Admit it. There have got to be times you enjoy the privilege." When Brett's eyes narrowed, as if he wondered whether he should be offended, Sunny added, "I would."

"But it all comes with a price," he warned. "There are obligations. And sometimes I'd just as soon do without them."

"But you've had the good life, and because of it I'll bet you've acquired certain expectations, certain attitudes and behaviors. Like playing rugby instead of football. Or choosing escargot over onion rings."

He smiled faintly, as if bored by her conjecture. "Now how do you know I like rugby?"

Sunny ignored his attempt to change the subject. "I don't. But for the life of me, I can't imagine why you'd want to give it up and walk away from such an existence."

Hazel set Sunny's cappuccino in front of her with a thunk, slopping it over the rim before she walked away. Brett pulled a napkin from the dispenser and automatically handed it to her.

Sunny reached for it, and when their fingers met, a spark of electricity went pinging up her wrist. The fine hairs on the back of her arm stood up.

Brett stared at her pensively, as if the touch that passed between them, and over a cheap paper napkin, had been enough to ignite and burn. An undercurrent of awareness sizzled.

Sunny's fingers, still smoldering, fumbled to dab at the spill. "Thank you. I—I don't want to get it on my skirt." She paused while the waitress put down the teapot, cup and sliced lemons, then left again. "And Brett? I wasn't trying to pry. Or even be critical. It's just..." She pushed the soiled napkin aside. "My parents were on the move a lot, and I haven't known very many people who have your kind of family history. Or that kind of security. It makes me wonder if you know what you're giving up."

Brett silently poured a cup of tea, then squeezed a bit of lemon into it. He wiped his fingertips, then crumpled the napkin, as she had done. "You'll have a few weeks to get an inside look at my life, with and without my title." Picking up a sugar packet, he ripped it open. He tapped a few grains into the tea, then stirred. "After my parents go home, you can give me your opinion. Should I barter myself away to a woman I don't love, in order to secure a place in society and a hefty inheritance? Should I make love to a woman I don't care about in order to secure an heir?"

Sunny shifted uncomfortably. The one thing her parents had taught her was unconditional love. Everyone needed it, deserved it.

Yet the life he alluded to seemed hollow, plastic, even devoid of emotion.

"Because," Brett continued, putting the spoon aside and lifting his cup from the saucer, "after you've given a convincing performance for my parents, it can all be undone. I can grow weary of you and break our 'engagement.'"

Uncertainty skittered up Sunny's spine. But she refused to give in to the ominous suggestion—the same way she refused to fall victim to Brett's piercing blue gaze. In some odd way she knew he was issuing her an ultimatum, and she felt she had to stand up to it.

"Fine. The day your parents go home and I move out of your apartment, I'll tell you exactly what I think you're giving up. And I won't mince words."

Brett lifted his cup in a mock toast. "I'm looking forward to it." He took a sip, then gazed at her steadily over the rim.

Unable to tear her eyes away, Sunny took a long, scalding draft of her cappuccino.

"Take it easy, luv. You're going to get burned," Brett warned.

"I've already been burned. I mean I—I did that purposely, to clear my head," she stated.

"And singe your tongue," he said wryly.

They both, implicitly, understood the double meaning.

She set the cappuccino aside. "Brett? Are you sure you want to go through with this? With me? Because if you've had second thoughts, and want to change your mind or find somebody else—"

"No second thoughts."

"If this blows up or backfires, or your parents figure it out, I don't want to be held accountable."

"Sunny, I think you're being a jolly good sport about the whole thing. If it doesn't play out like we planned, I won't be any worse off than I am now." He chuckled. "Of course, we're going to have to think about how to manage this at the office. I'll admit I mentioned it to Carmella and Emily. But Emily's a good friend of mine, so she won't say anything if we don't want her to. Carmella won't, either. I think we should keep up the status quo—a working relationship. That way there'd be no explanations."

Sunny laced her fingers around the cup of cappuccino. "I don't know you and you don't know me, right?"

"That's it. Nodding acquaintances," he confirmed.

"Hey, I'll just look the other direction when I see you coming," she volunteered, her insides twisting with what felt too much like rejection. Apparently she was good enough to be his fiancée, but not his friend. "If we meet in the hall, or share the same elevator or anything. I mean, we've never really talked before, so—"

"But there's the rub, Sunny," Brett admitted, his thumb stroking the rim of his teacup. "We really don't know anything about each other, and we should. Especially if we're going to convince my parents. Otherwise we'll make mistakes. Tomorrow's Friday," he murmured thoughtfully. "You could move in tomorrow night and we'd have the whole weekend—and all of next week—to get to know each other. What do you say?''

''Tomorrow night? I thought you were joking about that.'' Surprised, Sunny drew back. She hadn't imagined he'd want her around until the last minute. The upside of his offer was that it included seven more nights away from her parents and the way their eccentricities were taking over her apartment. ''If you have plans for the weekend, or dates next week, I'd be in the way. You'd have to explain me away.''

He offered up a toothy, irresistible smile. ''Not a problem.''

''You won't say I'm your American cousin, will you?''

''No, there won't be any explaining. My calendar's clear.''

Sunny debated. Even one less night of tofu and beans was appealing. ''Um, if I moved in early, that would have to include dinner, too,'' she bargained.

He lifted a shoulder as if the matter was inconsequential. ''I know a great restaurant where we can celebrate our first night together. I can make reservations there, or we can hang out at my place and throw steaks on the grill.''

''So you do eat red meat.''

He gazed at her, clearly puzzled. ''Is that an asset?''

''Definitely,'' Sunny confirmed. ''I'm not a vegetarian and I don't intend to be. I'll pack tonight. Because it looks like we have something in common, after all.''

Brett stood next to his car in the parking lot of the coffee shop. ''What?'' he asked. ''You didn't leave your car in the lot and walk over, did you?''

''Oh, no, I always take the bus to work.''

''Really?'' He appeared surprised by the information. ''Well, get in then. There's no sense in you taking the bus home.''

Sunny took an involuntary step back and waved him off. ''No, thanks. You probably have other things to do and—''

"Nothing but go back to the same apartment complex you're going to." Brett walked around the late model sports car and opened the door for her.

She hesitated. This was all happening too quickly. Tomorrow she was moving in with the office heartthrob. She'd just shared coffee—and tea—with him. And they'd actually touched—an unexpected contact that had left Sunny breathless, and quivery inside. The kind that put a great big question mark where her brains ought to be.

The thought of sitting beside him in the confines of that sporty little coupe, which was as blue as his eyes, made her go weak.

Sunny was not the kind of woman to rush into things. She methodically thought situations through, made logical decisions.

Yet here she was, swept away by a devil-may-care Englishman and his goofy scheme. She was moving into his life and jumping into the fancy leather passenger seat of his convertible as if she belonged there.

She reluctantly slid onto the seat, thinking luxury had never felt this good. The door closed after her with a quiet whoosh of air. She detected his clean, tangy scent, over and above the leather and the car polish.

"I didn't expect you to drive me home," Sunny said primly, as he put the car into Reverse.

"Don't be silly." He slipped a pair of reflective sunglasses on, then checked his rearview mirror.

From the corner of her eyes Sunny glimpsed the sunglasses, wondering if he was looking at her. She self-consciously adjusted the hem of her short skirt and tucked it under her thigh.

Brett's mouth twitched, but he stared straight ahead at the road.

"You can, um, just drop me off at the pool house." Sunny tried to sound casual, but the fact was she didn't want to run into her parents. She'd wind up explaining them to Brett—and then he'd have the last laugh.

He didn't answer, but expertly turned the car onto a main arterial. In less than five minutes they would be at the complex. "We may have to rethink our office game plan," he said.

"What? Why?"

"Because it looks like we'll be carpooling."

"Oh, no. I'll still take the bus," she protested.

"But what would my folks think if I drove to work and you took the bus?"

"That maybe you work late, or I work early, or..."

"I don't think so. They'd know in a minute I'd never let my fiancée ride the bus when I could share five minutes alone with her." He paused. "I've always thought being alone in a car with someone of the opposite sex is kind of...sexy. Don't you think?"

Sunny swallowed. "Sexy?"

He gave her a sideways glance. "You know, luv. The idea of being alone, encapsulated in a moving car. Music and conversation. Sitting shoulder to shoulder." He focused on the road, drumming his fingers on the steering wheel. "Of course, you Americans have a phrase for it—'fast cars, fast women.'"

"I guarantee this is one woman who is *not* in the fast lane," Sunny clarified. "In case you were wondering."

An amused smile spread over his face. "I dare say that is probably for the best."

A few moments slipped by before she realized he had intentionally hit a hot spot with her. One she'd have to address. "Speaking of parents," she began hesitantly, "I'd just as soon keep mine out of this."

"Oh?"

"Well, we might run into them, being in the same complex and all, and I'd just as soon not have that happen. I certainly don't want them to know I'm posing as your girlfriend."

"Fiancée," he corrected.

"Whatever." She waved her hand. "It's enough for

them to think I'm staying with a friend for a couple of weeks.''

''Okay. That's fine with me. If that's the way you want it.''

''I do.''

A moment later, Brett pulled off onto the side street adjacent to the apartments. Then, offering her a lopsided grin, he wheeled into the drive. Sunny clutched the armrest and pressed her shoulder blades into the bucket seat. She still slid into him.

''Don't you just love the way a sports car takes the curves and hugs the road?'' he asked drolly, letting the steering wheel spin back within his hands.

''Hugs?'' she repeated, pulling herself upright. ''I thought I was going to be in your lap.''

He passed the pool and clubhouse, and pulled up at the first intersection. She straightened her skirt again and unconsciously motioned for him to make a right, toward her apartment building.

''Of course, when we drive together you will need to hug me instead of the door,'' he said.

''I wasn't hugging the door,'' she argued. But the truth was she had intended to leave as much space between them as possible. ''And you can stop right here.''

Brett pulled into the first available parking space and threw the car into Park. He stripped his sunglasses off and tossed them on the dash. ''Back to *my* parents again, okay? They'll expect us to be lovey-dovey, you know. And they'll like your proper edge, as it will make the story all the more believable. But…''

''Yes?''

''How about a kiss?'' he suggested boldly, his gaze dropping possessively to her mouth. ''For you may find that you can't tolerate me. And that would be a pity, to put on a show for my mother and father, when you find me insufferable.''

''I—I never said you were insufferable.''

"Really?"

His gaze trailed over her curiously. He turned on the seat, leaning closer to her, then waited, giving her the opportunity to withdraw, to protest.

But she didn't—and for the life of her she didn't know why.

"Or we could say," he whispered, his breath fanning her cheeks, "that we'll share a kiss to seal the secret about who I really am."

"I won't tell," she promised, feeling dizzy as he loomed closer.

"Mmm. Good…" His mouth first nuzzled hers. His lips, so soft and warm and tasting of tea and lemon, almost surprised her. The tip of his nose brushed against hers, and raspy stubble scraped her cheek. He smelled seductively fresh, like salt and sea air.

When Sunny involuntarily kissed him back—her mind in a muddle, her senses on overload—Brett deepened the kiss, sending earth-shattering sensations through her. Her respiration grew shallow and her heart started to pound. And behind her eyelids she saw a panorama of stars. Shooting stars. Spinning stars. Dazzling waves of stars.

Sunny's hand went to his shoulder to steady herself, her fingers curving over the thick muscle there. His shoulders were so wide they seemed to envelop her, in a protective, supportive kind of way. Her fingertips inched upward, over the seam of his dress shirt. She discovered the warmth of his flesh above his starched collar and beneath his ear. The tip of her fingernail traced the neat edge of his haircut, the tiny hairs teasing the pad of her forefinger.

Brett flexed his shoulders, and groaned. He pulled reluctantly away, even as his mouth continued to taste hers.

Finally he broke the kiss and tipped his forehead against hers. "I do think we'll get on," he predicted softly. "My family should be suitably convinced that our affections are genuine. And if I didn't know better, I'd be nearly convinced of it myself."

Chapter Three

By the time she'd run up the two flights of steps to her apartment, Sunny was gasping—and it wasn't due to the exercise. No, the reason her head was spinning and her lungs had turned six shades of breathless blue, was because of Brett Hamilton.

He had kissed her until she ached—and she'd kissed him right back. She'd never realized a man could taste so good.

She'd never imagined she could lose herself like that. Not her. Not Sunny Robbins. She'd steeled herself to take cold, analytical views of everything life presented. That's why she worked so hard in her job as a paralegal. She could see both sides of a story, weigh issues and make rational decisions.

Never in her wildest dreams had she thought a man like Brett Hamilton could make her feel so light-headed and giddy.

The lyrics to a song popped into her head, and she shivered. "With just one kiss…"

Well, shiver me timbers, she thought insanely, *some English bloke, with a title and a reputation, plants a kiss on*

*me in the middle of the apartment parking lot, and I fall
apart like a sinking ship.*

She would put a stop to it. She swore she would. For a
moment, standing there on the commercial carpet outside
the door to her apartment, Sunny thought about who and
what she was.

Because she liked a roof over her head, and benefits that
included medical and dental, she held a nine-to-five job in
the corporate world. She ate commercially prepared meals
in throwaway boxes because it was efficient and convenient. She voted a straight Republican ticket, read the *New
York Times,* paid her taxes when they were due, and balanced her checkbook every week. She'd never been hauled
off to jail during a sit-in, a sit-down, a rally, protest or
demonstration. She didn't have a screaming room, and she
didn't paint abstract canvases of her inner self. She hadn't
dated anyone in two years and had only explored one
sexual experience. Love-ins were way out of her league.

It went without saying her parents thought they had
failed. On every count.

Then Brett Hamilton came along, proposed an absurd
charade, kissed her and swept her off her feet.

She looked down at her toes. Okay. She was still standing. Barely.

Sunny pivoted on her heels and sank back against the
wall, taking a cleansing breath. She would drive that mad-
dening man out of her mind by sheer will and determination. She swore she would.

Overhead, the fluorescent lights flickered. The scents of
honey and vanilla surrounded her, making her take deep,
gulping breaths, to get as much of the calming scent into
her lungs as she could. Inside, she heard her father's low
hum as he chanted, "Ommm…"

Damn, she thought irritably. He was meditating again.
Some days he was up at the crack of dawn, meditating and
searching for the soul of his universe. Sometimes it was
dusk—or before lunch, or after lunch, or after the eleven

o'clock news. She really, really hoped he found himself soon.

For to imagine him there, planted in the center of the living room in the lotus position, was one more reminder of why she was moving in with Brett: to resume her own orderly life.

She sighed heavily and fumbled with her key. She jammed the key in the lock, then winced and pushed the door open. "Mom? You left the door unlocked again."

Her father, in his striped shaman's robe, cracked one disapproving eye. His chanting grew louder, as if he could drive out any distractions by sheer willpower. "Ommm…"

Her mother wandered out of the kitchen, wearing her favorite cotton skirt and peasant blouse, a concho belt tightly girding her plump middle. Dressed in wool socks, her feet noiselessly scuffed the floor. She brushed her long, graying hair back from her face, but didn't look up from the recipe card in her hand. "Hi, dear," she said absently. "If people want in, they're going to get in. And if people want something bad enough to steal it, I say just give it to them. They must need it worse than we do."

"Mother, this isn't the commune," Sunny reminded her edgily, "and these are *my* things. I don't want to have to replace them."

"I know. It's just…" Her mother shrugged. "Old habits and old philosophies are hard to break."

"Ommm…" her father chanted.

"I know, I know," Sunny said, relenting. "I'm not trying to be difficult, but I worry about keeping everything nice, that's all." She threw her handbag on the table and moved to the kitchen, her nose twitching. The apartment did, she realized, smell better than the incense her father usually burned. "What smells so good? Are you baking?"

"It's vanilla," her mother said. "But it's for candles."

Sunny stopped stock-still in the doorway of her galley kitchen and stared. Her Cuisinart was in pieces. Cupboard doors hung open and the sink was heaped with utensils.

Discarded candle forms littered the countertops. Cork-stoppered bottles of scent cluttered her lazy Susan. On the stove, every one of her stainless steel pans had wax simmering in it.

Wax dribbled down the front of the stove. Wax speckled the floor. Wax puddled and dried on the chrome fixtures. It glopped in fascinating spatter patterns over the cherry-wood cabinets. It had apparently been sopped up with her brand-new kitchen towels.

A ripple of frustration mushroomed to a tidal wave. Sunny's head started pounding and her stomach churned. "Mother…?" Her one-word query was carefully contained, carefully executed.

"Beeswax, and all natural ingredients," her mother replied, as if that answered every question. "I couldn't find a candle in the house. And candles nurture the soul. They lend atmosphere. They save electricity."

"You can *buy* candles! At the store."

"Not like these," her mother said proudly, displaying a slightly unbalanced six-inch pillar.

Sunny gaped, and the pent-up frustration winching her shoulders tight popped like a spent balloon. One more unforgettable moment with her lovable, goofball parents. Sometimes it was just easier to give up than try to fight it. Her shoulders slumped. "No, definitely not like those," she agreed dryly. "And that would be, what? A wax takeoff on the Leaning Tower of Pisa?"

Her mother lifted the saucer of Sunny's good china a fraction of an inch higher and regarded the listing candle. "What do you know? Maybe I created a novelty."

"Maybe." Sunny reluctantly moved to the stove and tipped the smallest of the gourmet pans to check the contents. Sick-looking wax, half-congealed, purled to the other side. "Mom, do you have any idea what I paid for these pans?"

"Must have been a lot. They conduct a nice, even heat."

Sunny nodded mutely. "This," she said finally, "is an omelette pan. It used to cook eggs."

Her mother's face flickered with recognition. "Oh, honey, I'll bet you're hungry, aren't you? I got so wrapped up in what I was doing I completely lost track of time."

"That's okay," Sunny said, holding up a hand as she turned to the freezer. "Don't worry about it." She yanked open the appliance door and came face-to-face with a dozen more candles.

"Putting candles in the freezer before they're set creates a beautiful crackle pattern."

"Uh-huh. But what happened to the *food* that was in here?"

"Oh, honey, I just threw away a few of the things in the front that were freezer burned…or that had refined sugar, or a lot of additives…."

Sunny reached around the most beautiful of the crackled candles and pulled out a box. "Well, we still have these," she said happily, dumping the contents on the last clean plate. "I'll just nuke 'em."

From the corner of her eye, Sunny saw her mother take a step back and stare in horror at the forlorn-looking little chicken nuggets. "Oh, Sunny, no. That isn't good for you. The fat content alone in processed foods—"

Her father joined them in the kitchen. "Sunshine," he said reprovingly, "I don't think 'nuke 'em' is an expression we should use loosely. Doing so strikes a vein of terror in all third world countries."

Sunny momentarily put the heel of her hand to her forehead, where she knew the throbbing was about to start. "Daddy, whatever was I thinking? Some third world country probably has my kitchen bugged and now they know all about my plans to cook chicken nuggets."

Her father cocked his head at her, the way he always did when he was disgruntled, and his single earring winked at her. A loose strand of hair had come free from his ponytail and he hooked it behind his ear. "You really need to take the world situation seriously, Sunshine," he admonished.

"I'm sorry," she said. "But the only world situation I'm concerned with right at this minute is mine. I'm hungry and I'm tired, and I want to talk to you."

"Your father picked up fresh mustard greens at the co-op," her mother wheedled, her eyes fixed on the plate inside the microwave.

"Oh, yummy." Sunny automatically punched in the numbers on the appliance, and when it was humming she turned back to her parents. "Sylvia. Doug," she began, unconsciously lapsing into the psychobabble she'd learned many years ago, when she'd shared their living space in the California beach community. "I have the opportunity to move on, at least for a little while. A friend has offered me a bed and a place to chill. I have some life choices I want to ponder, and—"

"You aren't moving out on us, are you?" her mother exclaimed.

"Only for a little while. I just need my space."

"Space is relative," her father reflected. "The freedom of the spirit soars beyond the physical limitations."

"Doug," Sunny said to her father, her voice flat and no-nonsense, "I figured you could use the room. My apartment's kind of small."

"Honey, we're not going to be here forever." Her mother patted her arm consolingly. "We're only between places right now."

"Just until we find a place in Vermont."

"Because if we're in your way—"

"No, it's okay. I understand," Sunny assured them. She opened the refrigerator door to grab a soda and was immediately faced with dozens of votive candles cooling there. She closed the door and came away empty-handed. "I love you guys, I do. But the opportunity for a temporary roommate came up, and I just took it, that's all. I'm sure you'll still be here when I get back."

"I'm not so certain," her father warned. "The manager at the food co-op asked your mom about a job."

"A job? Really?" Hope spiraled, and Sunny tingled with anticipation.

"I told him about my homemade soap," she confided. "He wants to sell it."

The bubble of expectation quickly burst. Sunny pulled her plate of limp-looking chicken nuggets from the microwave. "So," she said. "Will you be needing the roaster or the stock pot for the soap?"

"Oh, don't worry about that," her mother scoffed. "You've got more than enough pans. I'm more concerned about getting the goat's milk. It's a hard ingredient to find, especially here in Boston."

"We get to Vermont," her father promised, his gaze settling lovingly on his wife, "you'll have your own goats."

Her mother slipped under his arm. "I have one old goat right now," she teased, poking him affectionately.

Sunny cringed. She couldn't imagine being chummy enough with Brett to say something so corny. "I'm moving out tomorrow," she said abruptly.

"So soon?" Her mother's disappointment was palpable.

"He said it would be a good time, and—"

"He?" her parents echoed, breaking slightly apart.

"Well…yes." Sunny eyed the chicken nuggets. Suddenly she wasn't so hungry anymore. She forced herself to pick one up and nibble at it. She hadn't meant to mention that her new roommate was a "he." Her parents openly expressed their concern that she spent more time on work than she did on her interpersonal relationships.

"That's different," her father said, his smile growing wide.

"Honey, you don't need to make any excuses for moving in with your boyfriend."

"He's *not* my boyfriend."

Her parents chuckled as if they didn't believe her.

"He's just a friend," she insisted. "Really. Besides, if I did have a boyfriend, the last thing I'd do was move in with him."

"Well, you know what they say, Sunshine," her father admonished, his expression smug. "If it feels right, do it."

Sunny lugged all her suitcases and boxes over to Brett's apartment by herself. Not because he wouldn't have helped, but because she had an ulterior motive. She was reluctant to have him to meet her parents—and she didn't want them to meet him. Not quite yet. They'd give him the third degree, she knew.

They definitely thought she had a "thing" for Brett Hamilton. The sly glances they kept giving her, the secret smiles they exchanged—it was unnerving, all of it.

By the time she got to Brett's she felt as if she was on exhibition. And this, she reminded herself, was just the beginning.

"This is all of it?" Brett asked dubiously, gazing at the motley collection of one pasteboard suitcase and three cardboard boxes. "You could be here for two weeks. Maybe three."

"I travel light," Sunny said. "My family never got bogged down with personal possessions."

"That part's nice. My family, on the other hand, got bogged down with too many of them," he confided, picking up the clothes she'd carried over on their hangers. "Here. I'll put these in the closet for you." He paused. "You know, I'd have been happy to help bring your things over."

"If I'd needed any help I would have asked. I'm not shy." *Liar.*

If she wasn't shy, why had she spent the day at Wintersoft ducking in doorways and furtively glancing down hallways? Because she'd wanted to avoid Brett Hamilton, that's why. She didn't know what to say to him. She didn't know how to act. Not with a man she didn't know, a man she'd agreed to move in with.

The entire premise was ridiculous. She must have taken leave of her senses.

"Really? You aren't?" Brett curiously raked a look down her, the hangers swinging from the V between thumb and forefinger. "People mistakenly think a man wants a shy, timid woman. But I've never thought that. Adventuresome, determined, maybe a little gritty. Someone who can make life interesting—now that's a woman who catches my eye."

Sunny pushed a smile onto her lips. "Yes, me moving in with you promises to be interesting. I guarantee your life is going to be an adventure from here on out."

"Maybe. But…" The fingertips of his free hand skimmed over the shoulder seams of her sweaters, suit jackets and blouses. "Your wardrobe is less than adventurous."

"Excuse me?"

"I had no idea there were so many shades of beige."

Sunny stopped. "And what's wrong with beige?"

"It's a bit…" he riffled through her fawn-colored power suit, an off-white blouse, dun skirt, tan dress pants and khakis "…well, dull, actually."

"They're neutrals. They go together. They go with anything."

He lifted a noncommittal shoulder. "Definitely classic cuts. I'll give you that."

"I don't need you to give me anything," Sunny blustered. "It's an understated look."

"Definitely." His voice lifted with a sliver of sarcasm. "And while my mother loves understated elegance, she also likes a little color."

"I'm not buying a new wardrobe to impress your mother."

"It's all right, luv. I'll buy it."

"You're not buying me clothes."

''My treat, Sunny. After all, what woman doesn't like to shop?''

''Me.''

He sighed in obvious exasperation. ''I only want this to work. I want you to feel comfortable, and to have an edge with my parents. I didn't mean to insult your choices or infer that your things aren't good enough. They are. It's just that I know what my mother likes.''

''You're going to dress me up like a doll.''

He grinned. ''I'd rather not. I don't have the time for it, and frankly, I don't think you'd stand for it.''

''Okay. Then you're going to trot me out like a show pony.''

He chuckled. ''All right. I'm going to show you off, yes. As my intended. And I want to give this the best possible advantage. Is there anything wrong with that? I want my parents' first impression to be smashing.'' Brett folded the clothes over his arm. ''Sunny, let's go shopping tomorrow. I'll use every wile and every opportunity to convince my parents you are just the girl for me. C'mon, now. You won't let Lady Harriet have at me, not over a few shirts and things, will you?''

''Brett. It seems…unnecessary.''

''We've got to do something, anyway. To get to know each other. We can make a day of it, spending my money at the mall.''

Sunny wavered. Brett was obviously willing to do whatever he had to to make this succeed. ''Oh, I suppose I could use a few things,'' she conceded.

''Just to play the part.''

''We aren't talking gloves and hats and those clunky purses you hang over your arm, are we?''

He laughed, hard enough to make his shoulders shake. ''That, my dear,'' he said, ''is the kind of thing I'm trying to avoid.''

The bedroom Brett offered her was exquisite. He hadn't scrimped on decorating, Sunny realized. The second bedroom of his apartment was twice as large as the only bedroom of hers. He had a four-poster bed in the room, and a footstool to get up on it. The armoire housed a television, and the walk-in closet was as big as her bath.

The comforter, in brilliant shades of garnet and indigo-blue, was four inches thick. The matching drapes at the windows were expertly swagged, falling in meticulous puddles of silk on the claret-colored carpet.

Brett stood in the doorway. "If there's anything you need..." He left the rest unsaid.

"This is more than I expected."

"I rather overdid it on the guest room. But I wanted my visitors to be comfortable." He paused. "I'm sorry there isn't a private bath."

"Brett, I know how to share."

He chuckled, as if she said something outrageously funny. "Maybe," he conceded. "But I don't."

"Ah, the lifestyles of the rich and famous..." Sunny tried to look busy by arranging two bottles of lotion on the dresser.

Brett strolled in, taking note of her unpacked boxes. "And this would be...?" He picked up the blue-tinted lotion, then screwed off the cap and took a whiff. "Blueberries 'n Crème? Sounds like dessert. Mmm, smells even better." He tipped the bottle and poured a small amount in the palm of his hand. "Give me your arm. I need to know what you smell like after hours."

Sunny instinctively drew back. "I don't think so."

"Come along. Body chemistry and all that. It changes."

Sunny didn't move.

"My parents would expect me to know, I suppose, that you like this blueberry stuff over, say, strawberry. Or—" he leaned down and peered at the second bottle "—lemon ice." He made the smallest beckoning gesture.

Sunny's intentions to keep him at arm's length buckled.

Her elbow drifted away from her side and she slowly, tentatively, extended her hand.

Sliding his palm under her wrist, Brett turned her arm over, until the soft inner side was exposed. Inside, Sunny started quivering, her blood began pounding and her senses went on high alert.

He feathered the lotion over her pulse point, letting it soak into the skin. Then he stroked it with his thumb, releasing the scent and heating her flesh. A prickling sensation shimmied up Sunny's arm, and Brett unwittingly followed the ticklish path, to her elbow. Sunny's heart hammered harder as his hand slid back down, massaging the lotion into her arm.

"Smooth," he commented.

"What?" Sunny asked breathlessly, lifting her wrist off his hand. "The way you accomplished that?"

Brett's eyes crinkled with amusement. "No. The lotion, I meant." He leaned so close Sunny was sure the tip of his nose would stroke her flesh. "Very nice. I do believe I'll tell my mum most nights you smell like a blueberry tart." When he lifted his head, his eyes were twinkling. "You know, something mushy like that."

Sunny choked. "A tart? A blueberry tart?"

"Well, we'll have to say silly little things like that, don't you think?" His lower lip twitched as he baited her. "As for me, you can just rave about my smashing good looks. I got my eyes from my mother's side of the family. She'll be pleased if you notice."

It was the only invitation Sunny needed to consider Brett's deep-set eyes. His irises were as faceted as a precious gem, the pupils black as onyx. The lashes framing them were as dark and thick as a sable brush, and she vaguely wondered if he'd shut them when he'd kissed her. "Your mother's side of the family bequeathed you something precious," she said finally. "I'll remember to comment on it."

He smiled, one side of his mouth riding higher than the

other. "Come on. Enough of this foolishness. Dinner's on the table. Steaks as you requested, and everything that goes with it."

"Am I supposed to tell your mother that you cook?"

"Please do."

Sunny was surprised to discover he'd set the table with linen napkins. An open bottle of wine was on the table. When Brett walked around and pulled the chair out for her, she stopped and stared at him, then looked at the seat. She couldn't remember the last time someone had pampered her with those kind of manners. Her parents didn't buy into gender-based behaviors.

"We've got to practice," he explained. "For when we go out. So it looks like we do this all the time."

Sunny moved stiffly to the chair, eventually sitting as if she was perched on a dozen eggs. She waited until he sat before unfolding her napkin. "You plan to be this attentive?" she asked. "For the whole week?"

He inclined his head. "It won't kill me."

"Not if it gets the job done, right?"

He smiled mysteriously. "And then again, it's the proper thing to do. I think you'll find my family does like to make sure things are proper."

Sunny rolled her eyes. "Then I guess they'll have a real fit about us living together, won't they?"

"Most likely," he admitted. "But you and I will know we aren't doing anything wrong."

Then why did Sunny have the feeling that they *should?* If it was just an inclination on her part, she needed to get over it. Quickly.

"So," she said, changing the subject and smoothing the napkin over her lap, "do you always have wine with dinner?"

"Most nights." He offered her the salad. "My parents will expect it, by the way. They usually like a nice cabernet. Keep in mind, I never drink a dry wine. Usually sweet."

"Never dry, usually sweet," Sunny repeated, putting the tongs back in the salad bowl and handing it to him.

"What about you?" he prompted.

"Me?" Sunny knew she looked surprised. "Oh, I—I'm not picky."

"Name something."

She hesitated, and finally decided honesty was the best policy. "I can't. The only wine I ever drink is the generic cheap stuff in big bottles."

He poured a small amount in her flute and smiled. "See if you like this."

She picked it up and, looking over the rim at Brett, sampled. He waited expectantly for her verdict. "It's fine." A second slipped away. "Really."

His mouth twitched. "What would you like instead?"

"Water? With lemon?"

He rubbed a knuckle over the stubble on his cheek and grinned. "So much for gourmet tastes," he said, a low rumble of appreciation rumbling through his chest. "I'm disappointed. That wine was forty dollars a bottle, and it didn't impress you."

"I didn't come here to be impressed, Brett."

There was a wicked glint in his eye and a taunt on his lips. "What did you come here for, then?"

"The free room and board."

Brett stopped in surprise, then laughed out loud and shook his head. "Emily once said you were honest to a fault. I'm actually relieved you didn't come here for me. That kind of thing gets tedious."

After seeing that she had water—and lemon—Brett contentedly filled his own flute and began to converse with her. It amazed Sunny how easily he talked. She was certain the man was half politician. She couldn't imagine him not being able to talk his way out of anything, including an arranged marriage.

It occurred to her vaguely that she was like a stage prop

in a play: something to look at and help make the action move along.

For the rest of the evening she had that feeling about how she fit into the apartment and Brett's life. When he finally said he had to make some phone calls, Sunny was more than happy to retire to her room. Her *own* room.

After midnight, when all was quiet, she ventured across the hall to the apartment's only bath. To her horror, Brett stepped out of his room at precisely the same moment. He wore a baggy pair of sweatpants that rode low on his hips and sagged below his belly button. In the half-light, his torso was an inviting ripple of muscle.

Sunny's gaze reluctantly traveled up the hollow of his bare breastbone and over his sculptured chest to the full, angular cut of his shoulders. Men like this, she thought insanely, with their hair loose and mussed, their skin bronzed and damp-looking, loomed on the movie screen. They sold products in magazines. Or hung guitars around their necks and wooed millions of female fans. They didn't share apartments with Sunny Robbins.

They both stood there for a few uncomfortable seconds, looking at each other.

"Sorry," he apologized finally. "I'd just gotten out of the shower and realized I'd left some of my things in here."

"I...couldn't sleep," she offered lamely.

His smile grew. "Probably all that color keeping you awake."

"Excuse me?"

"The pajamas," he said, his eyes lighting on her red-and-yellow flannel pajamas. "I see you do have *some* color in your wardrobe."

Sunny cringed, imagining how she must look in her faded, stretched-out favorite pajamas. She toughed it out, though, and offered him the first offhand remark that went zinging through her head. "My mother calls them the comfort food for my nocturnal soul—when she isn't nagging at me to get rid of them."

"Smart woman, your mother."

"Not necessarily. You probably haven't heard that American saying, 'Red and yellow, catch a fellow...'?"

She watched in fascination as his right eyebrow slowly lifted.

"Sorry, no. But my guess is that a bloke would be a lot easier to catch with something..." he trailed off indecisively, his gaze burning holes through the nubby flannel "...sexier?"

Chapter Four

Brett knew he shouldn't have said anything about Sunny's sleepwear. It should have been off-limits. But the truth was, he couldn't help himself. He wanted to know what was *under* that god-awful pair of pajamas.

Ever since she'd agreed to pose as his fiancée, he'd wondered what she'd look like in something other than lifeless colors. He sensed a vibrancy that Sunny willingly repressed—and he couldn't fathom it.

Those pajamas he'd caught her in had been priceless. He couldn't get the image out of his head for two hours afterward. Looking like a forlorn little waif, she'd stood there, cornered in the hall, in hideous flannel pajamas that puddled around her feet and hung over her shoulders. The sleeves had been too long and the neckline too big. Against the slim column of her throat, the garment had fallen away, to reveal the smallest patch of bare skin above her breast.

In the dim hall light, her creamy skin had had a porcelain quality. It had taken all the control he could muster to stop himself from straightening Sunny's collar, from running his fingertip over that tantalizing flesh. The longing to sate his curiosity and touch her was overwhelming.

He'd made a remark about sexier nightwear, but it was a guise, really, to cover his own discomfort. He'd have to insist on her finding something else, though, for if his mother stumbled across that pair of flannels, she'd know the engagement was all a ruse.

Unless, of course, Sunny only wore the tops...

The vision was unsettling. That top would barely cover her...

He shook his head and stared straight ahead, at the road. Damn, she had the curviest legs.

"You aren't a morning person, are you?" Sunny asked. "You haven't said two words since we left the apartment. Or have you changed your mind about the shopping?"

"No, I haven't changed my mind," he said briskly, turning onto the service road for the shopping mall. "Just thinking about all that's happened these past two days."

"You're wondering if it's worth it, trying to pass me off as your fiancée?"

"No. I was not wondering that." He pulled into the first available parking space, switched off the ignition and turned on the seat to face her. His gaze trailed over her jacket and slacks. "Frankly, I'm wondering where we're going to start with this transformation."

She pulled a face. "I should be insulted."

"But you aren't." He winked at her, intentionally using every ounce of male charm he possessed. "Because this is going to be fun."

"Then why do I feel like the sacrificial lamb?" she retorted.

"Free room and board, Sunny," he murmured, getting out of the car. "Keep reminding yourself that's why you're living with me."

He steered her into a huge department store and went to the upscale women's section, where they carried designer labels with commensurate price tags.

Sunny picked up a tailored blouse and visibly blanched at the cost.

Brett took the hanger out of her hand and put it right back on the rack. "No more beige," he ordered.

"It's tan."

"I don't care." He pulled a cranberry suit off a four-armed display. "Try this."

"Red?"

His mouth wobbled, but he refused to grin. "I got enough of a glimpse last night to know you look particularly good in red." Sunny glanced away, obviously discomfited. "A size eight. Will it do?"

She took the hanger from him. "Close enough."

"And something in blue," he said thoughtfully. "Royal-blue." She glanced back over her shoulder at him, and the pose made his heart clench.

"Only you," she accused, "would pick colors that have titles attached to them."

His mouth curled sardonically as he handed her a blue dress.

A saleswoman fluttered to their side, taking the garments from Brett and Sunny. "I'll put these in a dressing room for you," she offered. "Until you're ready."

Brett, much to Sunny's dismay, continued to waltz through the department, heaping the salesclerk's arms with his finds. "This is going to take all day," Sunny finally complained.

"I know, darling," he soothed, his response exaggerated for the salesclerk's benefit, "and you're going to get your hair mussed. But it's such fun to pamper you."

"What *are* you doing?" Sunny demanded under her breath.

"I'm practicing being attentive. For my parents."

"Well, you're overdoing it," she muttered, vaguely aware how other shoppers, all women, were devouring Brett with hungry eyes. She knew in that instant how many would happily trade places with her.

"Sir," the saleswoman cooed, "can I get you a beverage while your wife tries these on?"

Sunny couldn't stand it. "We're not married," she said.

"Yet." Brett loosely draped an arm around her with a wicked gleam in his eyes. "But we're...*engaged.*"

"Not officially."

"Next week," he crooned as Sunny stared at him. He dragged his attention away to answer the salesclerk. "And yes to the beverage. A soft drink? Anything will do."

When she scurried away, Sunny turned on him. "Why on earth are you doing this?"

"It just occurred to me. I wanted to see if you feel as uncomfortable being forced into an 'arranged marriage' as I do just thinking of it."

Sunny lifted her hand. "Okay, okay. A point well taken. And you really didn't need to make the point at all, because I said I'd help you."

"But it doesn't seem as if you're having any fun while you're at it. Don't you like anything I've picked out? You keep shaking your head and putting everything back."

"Everything's...nice," she said slowly, realizing she didn't want to hurt his feelings. "But I'll never need all those things, and it seems like such a waste. Why, you must have picked out a dozen different outfits."

"You'll need something different for every day, to go to work in, and for every night of the week they're here."

"This is going to cost you a small fortune."

"I have a small fortune," he confessed, his voice filled with indifference. "Until they lop it off and cut me off from my inheritance. So. What does it matter if I spend it now?"

"You should be spending it on yourself. Not on me. Not on someone you don't even know."

His eyes went to half-mast, as if he was unaffected by her earnest arguments. "Who knows? Maybe the money will be well spent as a good investment. In my future—and yours."

If there was any deeper meaning in Brett's words, Sunny

chose to ignore it. He sank into the chair the salesclerk indicated, a huge leather monstrosity with magazines and newspapers arranged on an adjacent side table.

The dressing room was enormous. Sunny, who had grown up getting her clothes from secondhand stores or discount outlets, was accustomed to standing behind a saggy, baggy drape and bumping her elbows against the thin walls of a squalid cubicle. Here, she had a cheval mirror, a tufted bench and an overstuffed chair. Instead of pins and needles, dirty tissues and paper tags littering the floor there was only plush carpet. The subtle scent of potpourri permeated the room.

Sunny had tried on two suits when Brett's voice drifted through the door. "If I'm paying, you have to model for me."

She zipped up the skirt to the cranberry suit. "Brett..."

"It's only fair. A man wants to know what he's paying for."

"Brett, hush." She pulled on the jacket, buttoning it in double time. "Okay. I'll be out in a minute." She hurried to the door, more intent on shutting him up than pacifying him with a modeling session.

She stepped out to find him sprawled in the chair, one ankle across his other knee. When she looked down at him, he cocked his head to one side. "That I like," he approved. "You can wear it for dinner. Or when we pick up my parents from the airport."

Sunny turned in front of the mirror and balanced on her toes, checking the hem length. She saw Brett's gaze dart to her knees, travel down the back of her calf and pause briefly on her heel, then make the journey back up again. He levered himself out of the chair to stand behind her. "I don't think I have the right shoes...." Her voice trailed off as his hands settled on her shoulders. She could actually feel his heat against her back, and when his hands slid down her upper arms she shivered.

"We'll find you pumps. Sensible pumps."

Brett had remarked yesterday about the sensible shoes she wore to work. It was fast becoming a private joke. Without them intending it to happen, their eyes collided and held in the mirror. For a second Sunny's breath caught, and she couldn't get any oxygen in or out of her lungs. He had the bluest eyes. And they were positively mesmerizing.

"My parents are known as Lord Arthur and Lady Miriam," Brett stated pensively, his voice going low, husky, "and I do believe I'll introduce you to them as Sunny, my lady in red."

They'd had moments like that all day. Pleasant moments. Moments when Sunny nearly forgot who Brett was, when she almost liked him for the person he was. When she was very, very attracted to him.

"Lunch," he declared after they had filled the trunk of his car with her new wardrobe. "Then we'll do the incidentals."

He'd whisked her away to a restaurant where there were club chairs and white linen napkins. They'd loitered over appetizers and mixed drinks. Brett ordered an extravagant meal of penne pasta, sautéed vegetables and slivers of chicken. For some perverse reason Sunny expected him to pick at it, but he didn't. He ate with relish, and she watched him, imprinting details into her memory: the way his elbows wedged against the table, the way he buttered a roll. The way he picked up his drink, tilting it toward her as he talked.

"Do you realize," she said finally, "that everyone in the restaurant is watching you?"

"Me?" he said, obviously surprised and looking around.

"Must be your commanding presence," she replied, trying to make a joke out of it. "Tell me, Brett. I've seen the way you handle people. I've seen the way people take to you. When we walked down the hall in your apartment building today, three different women said hello to you.

Why didn't you ask one of them—any one of them—to pose as your fiancée?''

He grew serious and feigned concentration before signing the check with a flourish. "When this all came about," he said slowly, "it was rather impulsive. I honestly thought that if I offered my brother a woman, any woman, he'd quit harping about my duty to get married. I suppose I could have looked around for someone to fit the bill...but you were there, and you seemed perfect for the job."

"Perfect for the job," she repeated.

"Okay." He shrugged. "I like your office demeanor. I certainly couldn't pick anyone at work who had designs on me. That wouldn't be fair, would it?"

"No, I suppose not." Sunny guiltily toyed with her fork, realizing that whether she wanted to admit it or not, her heart was inexplicably gravitating toward him. Okay, she knew it, but she refused to let it happen. "Brett, what about Emily? The boss's daughter is a knockout. She's got it all—brains, beauty, style. And she seems to have given up on finding her soul mate. She could be the other half of a perfect, no-strings-attached marriage."

"But I don't want to get married, Sunny." Brett pulled on his leather jacket. "That's the point." He paused. "Emily is someone I could trust, but I don't think she would have agreed to this little charade. Especially after the Todd Baxter fiasco. Besides, you..." He thoughtfully picked up his credit card and tapped it against the tabletop before picking up the receipt. "Well, I realized that you'd be perfect. You seem content with your job, your life. You don't appear to be desperately searching for your soul mate, doing the singles scene or being overly absorbed with self-improvement. So many women I meet these days are."

Something inside Sunny wilted. Brett wanted someone who wouldn't present a complication in his life. He had no idea that she was working toward a more stable life—or that she went fluttery inside every time he was near, every time they touched. "You thought," she said slowly, "that I'd never be a threat to your plans."

"That, and you work as a paralegal. You keep everyone's secrets." He winked at her, lowering his voice. "I figured you'd keep mine. Just like Emily and Carmella."

Sunny mutely watched him fold the receipt and slip it inside his wallet.

"Everything about you is perfect, Sunny. You're dependable, hardworking and trustworthy. You're exactly what I need to convince my parents I've made a responsible choice." Brett stood and put his wallet in his back pocket.

Sunny set her napkin back beside her plate and took one last calming sip of her drink. She reached for her coat, but Brett already had it open, to help her on with it.

Inside, she ached to make a flippant, self-deprecating remark—about her being as interesting as a ham sandwich, maybe, or as functional as a paper clip—but she couldn't bring herself to do it. Brett apparently didn't realize that he'd poked at her pride and wounded her self-esteem. Yet he was gallant enough to hold her coat. He was aware when her drink needed to be refilled or when she needed pepper instead of salt.

"So even though you did it impulsively, you made a conscientious choice," Sunny commented as they walked out the door.

"I guess I did. Yes."

"The bad thing is," she warned him, "that you made it with a conscientious objector. Pretending to be engaged, and taking part in this ruse, goes against my values. It isn't right, Brett. But of course, I don't think it's right for anyone to tell you who you should marry, either."

"Thank you for that."

"Of course, I'd pity the woman who does marry you— and has to shoulder your title and your situation."

"Really?"

"Well, you've made it quite apparent it's a millstone around your neck."

His stride faltered, and for a moment he fingered the center button on his jacket. "I suppose I have, haven't I? You must think I'm the spoiled little rich boy—but, Sunny, I try not to be. The fact is I have a very good life, and when I can I try to spread it around a little bit."

"Like that spending spree this morning?"

"Well, it wasn't all bad, was it?"

Try as she might, Sunny couldn't hold back a conciliatory smile. "It was decadent, all of it. And I've never felt so good spending someone else's money."

He laughed at her honesty. "And we're not done yet," he warned.

"Let's just window-shop," she said, reining in another surge of emotion. "I'm beginning to feel guilty. Like I'm taking advantage of you."

"I'm savvy enough to know when someone's taking advantage of me, Sunny. And when someone's with me because of who I am, or because of my title. I know you're not." They walked a few yards and paused in front of a home-decorating store. The window was filled with candles and lamps, pillows and throws. "Window-shopping's good. Side by side, talking about the things you like, the things you don't. Now me? I like to burn a lot of candles in the winter."

Sunny studied the fancy assortment of holiday candles. "My mother is into candles," she remarked.

"You're not?"

She repressed the smile that was threatening to play on her lips. Her mother was a character. She made life interesting, fun and exasperating. Sunny debated, wondering how much to reveal about her parents. "My mom's pretty unconventional, Brett. I suppose you'll meet her eventually. She just does things. This week she *made* candles."

"Really? How quaint."

"Quaint? In my gourmet kitchen? With my brand-new stainless steel pans?"

"Oh."

"Everything in the apartment smelled like vanilla. Even the chicken nuggets I had for dinner that night."

Brett looked faintly amused. He started walking, slowly drifting to the next store. "Is that why you smelled so good when you moved in?"

"You noticed?"

"Pretty hard not to. I'd rather hoped you baked cookies in your off hours."

Sunny winced. She didn't dare tell him some of the unconventional ingredients her father added to his favorite cookie recipe. "Oh, look," she said, changing the subject. "A leather store. My purse is shot, and your mother will be able to tell in a New York minute it's hand-me-down vinyl. Maybe we ought to look."

Brett scanned the display, which was fraught with silver studs, buckles and fringe. "Biker leather? I think not. It doesn't even look like you." He kept walking. "Now, here's something that does look like you...." He paused. Directly in front of an exclusive lingerie store.

Sunny's cheeks flamed.

He pulled open the door expectantly, waiting for her to enter. "I realized last night that your—" his gaze drifted to the lavishly hand-painted sign overhead "—'Intimate Apparel'—needs some updating."

Sunny stalled, staring into a mother lode of itty-bitty panties, lacy push-up bras and slinky, sexy nightwear. She wore functional white cotton undergarments. No fuss, no muss...and very uninteresting.

"Can't let my mother catch you in your flannels," he chided. "Not if we're going to keep up appearances."

"Brett..." Sunny glanced over his shoulder and realized they were holding up traffic by standing in the doorway. In that split second it occurred to her that she really wasn't any different than the other women entering the store. She'd merely *chosen* to wear the basics—just as they chose to wear something more interesting. Inside, the soft colors beckoned, the vivid ones taunted and teased.

Sunny was vaguely aware when several shoppers walked around her and into the store. Without thinking, she moved inside, too. But ten feet inside the shop, behind a rack of raw silk undies, she turned on her heel to face Brett. "It makes me nervous to think you could know what I have on *under* my clothes."

He looked down at her, even as one of his eyebrows lifted. "Maybe. But at least this way I won't be guessing." He pointed over her shoulder to the most provocative nightgown in the store. In ruby-red satin, it had spaghetti straps, a plunging neckline and a single slit to the thigh. "How about if you model that for me? Just to see if it fits."

Sunny's chin lifted defiantly. "In your dreams."

He feigned disappointment. "I was afraid that was the way it was going to be. In my dreams it is, then. Because that'll be one garment that's hanging in your closet."

Chapter Five

Brett peered at the hem of Sunny's new fuzzy robe. The plush garment was a trade-off for the sexy red nightgown he insisted she buy. And it wasn't fair. Because now he really *was* wondering what she had on beneath it.

She moved across the kitchen, getting two spoons, while he opened the cartons of ice cream. There it was again. The sheen of black leather.

"What in the world are you wearing under that?" he asked in frustration.

She stopped, leveling him with a flat stare as she pointed the spoon at him. "I told you you'd ask."

"I meant on your feet."

"Oh. That." Sunny let one shapely ankle slither between the folds of her new robe. Brett got a hitch in his groin, just imagining the curve of her calf, the long, lanky length of her leg. "My new pumps. I wanted to break them in."

"I see." He didn't see at all, at least not nearly as much as he wanted to.

"I pretty much grew up in Birkenstocks. My mom would

have a fit if she saw me wearing these things now. She'd say I was crippling my feet.''

Brett frowned. ''How do they feel?'' he asked quickly.

''Fine. I like the way they sound when I walk.'' She tapped the sculptured heel on the floor. ''Sensible shoes squeak. These—''

''Make their own kind of music,'' he finished for her.

''How,'' she said, offering a spoon to him in exchange for her carton of Death by Chocolate, ''did you know that?''

''Because I've been listening.''

She took a bite of the ice cream. ''I suppose you listened to how long I let the shower run after we got back from shopping, too.''

''Actually, I did. But only because I'm conscious of someone else being in the apartment. I figured you were either trying to avoid me or give me some space.''

''Neither one. I was enjoying the luxury of the bathroom. I love bathtubs. We never had a tub when I was growing up. So now I shower, then I soak.''

''I know what we forgot to buy,'' he said. ''Bubble bath. So it looks convincing that a woman lives here.''

''A bar of soap is all we need. My mother made our own soap.''

He leaned back against the counter, assessing her. He slowly took a bite of ice cream, his cheeks going concave as he savored it. ''Sunny?'' he said finally, thrusting the spoon back in the carton, ''are you always this practical?''

''Is that wrong? A fault, I mean?''

''No. I...'' He didn't quite know how to answer. The truth was he wasn't used to women who didn't try to amuse him, or wheedle their way into his heart and his pocketbook. Most women would have plopped a couple of fur coats on the counter while they were shopping, and gazed at him with huge, pleading eyes. Sunny, on the other hand, had picked out a tailored, navy-blue wool number. Something she claimed she'd always wanted. Something she could *use.* "I just think you'd want to indulge yourself. Occasionally."

"I suppose your parents will expect me to be a bit more…frivolous."

"Not necessarily. I merely think you'd want to be."

"My parents didn't put much value on material things. Some of it rubbed off."

"And some didn't?" He pulled out a bar stool and sat at the counter, waving a hand for her to join him.

Sunny lifted her robe and eased up onto a second stool. He heard two clunks and guessed she'd shed her pumps, probably to hook her feet around the rungs. "You've already figured out I didn't have a traditional upbringing. We moved around a lot, and I was home-schooled most of the time. I never got to know what it was like to be in a school play or have recess on a playground. My parents didn't believe in commercialism, or sexism, so getting the latest fashion doll was totally out of the question. I've sort of picked the things I've wanted—and maybe missed—and blended it with the values they've given me. So. When you say 'bubble bath,' the first thing I think of is my mother's concern about contaminating the groundwater, and her pre-occupation with natural ingredients. Or my father's dia-tribes on our economic support of manufacturers who take advantage of our natural resources and employ cheap labor and packaging practices in third world countries."

He pursed his lips. "My. You have all that to worry about? Just over bubble bath?"

"It adds up," she said seriously. "Kind of like everybody using hair spray and depleting the ozone layer."

He wanted to laugh. He did. But her earnest expression stopped him cold. Sunny Robbins carried the weight of the world on her shoulders. She denied herself things and looked deeply into issues. He wondered vaguely what it would take to make her laugh, to truly enjoy life. "I should warn you," he said. "My mother never has a hair out of place. In fact, her hair looks like it's been starched and stapled to her head. But I love her anyway.''

''Brett, I'm not here to judge.''

He nodded, believing her. ''Twenty questions,'' he suggested. ''What was your favorite toy—since you couldn't have the fashion doll?''

''Let's see. I got a bead-making kit once. My parents were trying to develop my creative side.'' She took a bite of ice cream. ''And you?''

''A pony when I was six.''

''A pony? You got a *pony,*'' she asked in disbelief, her spoon falling into the carton.

''Cocoa, a shetland pony. For my sixth birthday.''

''You lived every child's dream.'' She paused, her lower lip jutting slightly forward. ''I suppose you had dogs, too.''

Brett identified the tinge of envy in Sunny's voice and altered his reply. He knew she thought he already had too much. ''My father kept several hunting dogs, and my mother had some frothy little thing that sat on her lap all the time and yapped and made a nuisance of herself.''

''Your father hunts.''

''For sport.''

''Oh, God, no.''

''Excuse me?''

''I…'' Sunny looked away ''…was just thinking. About wildlife preservation.''

''Oh.'' Two seconds slipped by. ''Let me guess. One of your mother's—or father's—favorite causes.''

''Mother's.''

''Mmm. We won't bring up the hunting thing then, not with my father.'' He looked at her brightly. ''And me? Hey, I don't hunt.''

She looked at him with hope in her eyes, as if he'd just redeemed himself. ''Well…what do you do then? Just so I know.''

''Me…? I don't know. I guess I'm the social one of the family. I like to try new things and go new places. I love to sail and windsurf. In fact, if I didn't enjoy my job so much I'd probably be a beach bum.'' Sensing a flicker of alarm, Brett wondered if he said something wrong. ''You don't like the water.''

''Oh, no. I do. But I've never been on a big boat, and I've never sailed. It's just…''

''Yes?''

''We spent a lot of time on the beach when I was growing up. My memories of it aren't the best. People would come and go. They'd drift in and out of our life. There was a feeling of aimlessness about the summers I spent on the beach, and they're something I still can't shake.''

''What would you have had instead?''

''Me? Oh, I liked those little white houses with shutters. The ones that had a fenced yard in the back and maybe a swing set.''

''Ah, very traditional.''

''My parents say I'm a throwback to an earlier generation. They used to laugh and say they brought the wrong baby home from the hospital. But of course, they didn't, because I was born in—'' She stopped short, looking startled, as if she'd unintentionally said too much.

''In what?'' he prompted. ''Come on. You can't leave me hanging like this.''

Sunny scraped a bit of ice cream off the edge of her carton. ''In a teepee,'' she said slowly, quietly, as she slanted a cautious gaze at him. Brett forced himself to remain impassive. ''During a natural childbirth, with an herbalist and a shaman in attendance.''

''Oh. My. That was rather unconventional, wasn't it?''

Sunny lifted a shoulder noncommittally. ''My grandparents were horrified. They called me their little papoose for years afterward.'' He laughed. ''Brett, you have to understand, my parents are very unconventional people.''

''But they sound interesting,'' he pointed out. ''And fun. I'm anxious to meet them.''

But Sunny didn't offer an invitation. Instead, she said, "Tell me about your parents. So I'll know what to expect."

"My father worked long hours when I was growing up. I don't remember ever taking a do-nothing vacation, not like you did on the beach. But they liked long weekends, where we met people my father did business with, or attended events—mostly to be seen, or to stay in certain social circles. My mother gets quite flighty about her social calendar and invitations. She actually takes to her bed if she suspects she and father won't be included on particular guest registers."

"You're kidding!"

"Mother's reputation hangs on how many times she's named in the society columns," Brett confessed glumly. "My brother's wedding wasn't a celebration, it was an *event.* My father viewed it as an extravaganza to groom prospective business transactions. My mother saw it as an obligation to outdo, outspend and outentertain every one of her friends. And still people clamored to be on the guest list. It's a mystery to me. Frankly, I thought the bride and groom were lost in the lunacy of it all."

"And that's why you say you're not getting married."

"I don't need a show, if that's what it means. And I certainly don't need some woman with a pedigree." When Sunny lifted her eyebrows, he added, "I always thought marriage was about two people who chose to commit themselves to each other for a lifetime."

"Thoughts like that, Brett," she warned softly, "will crimp your playboy image."

"My what?"

"You know. The playboy image you have. The way you always tease and joke around."

"I like to tease and joke around. It shouldn't mean anything."

"Yes, well, I'm afraid it does. You've probably got a dozen women at Wintersoft wondering about you."

"I'm not 'wondering' about them."

"That's interesting," she said. "Because I'll bet not one of them knows about your serious side. Or even that you have one." She slid off the bar stool and slipped back into her pumps, swaying slightly. She picked up her empty carton of ice cream to put in the garbage pail under the sink. "I've got to say good-night," she said. "It's been a long day, and sometimes all this information about you bewilders me."

"You think you're the only one?" he retorted, a teasing light in his blue gaze. "Sometimes I sit back and wonder who I brought home from the office."

The weekend had evoked a myriad of conflicting emotions. Sunny had tossed and turned Saturday night. She'd thought about everything Brett had said, everything he'd done. He'd made her laugh, even when she didn't want to. He'd made her ponder, certainly when she'd rather not. He was an intriguing specimen of virility, of all-male taunt and torment. He had the kindest, most unexpected qualities, as well.

He'd said he'd chosen her because he could trust her—but the strangest thing was she felt as if she could trust him, too. With all her secrets, with all the longings she'd harbored throughout her life. She'd never told anyone about the summers on the beach, in that commune in Southern California. Yet she'd told Brett. She never told anyone about her parents' crazy philosophies about the environment or politics, or their day-to-day idiosyncrasies. Yet she had Brett. She'd never told anyone how she'd longed to have a baby doll to love and hold and dress and play with—or a fashion doll—for she'd expect people to remind her that such playthings created gender-based expectations and limitations. Yet she'd told Brett.

And not once had he been judgmental or rude. He never made her feel uncomfortable. He simply accepted her answers. About her family and herself.

Of course, that was easy, she guessed. He only had to

tolerate her crazy background for a few weeks. He certainly wasn't investing in it.

But his replies and comments intrigued her. She'd never once thought that, other than trying to escape the confines of marriage, he could have much of a value system regarding the institution—but apparently he did. He was firm in his belief that marriage was a sacred union between two people, not something to be taken lightly and made into a social circus.

He'd won a bit of her respect, and now she didn't know what to do with these unexpected feelings.

Sunday had been miserably wonderful. He'd taken her to breakfast, and she'd caught herself trying not to stare when he put sugar in his tea or ketchup on his eggs. He'd ask questions and she found herself trying to give bland replies. Suddenly she didn't want to give away too much of herself, and didn't want too much in return. Because she was beginning to like him—and that couldn't happen. It couldn't happen at all, because when all was said and done, she'd be alone again…and she'd start wondering one more time what she had missed out on in life.

Her feelings were all mixed up when she got ready for work Monday morning. She heard Brett in the shower and did everything she could to avoid him in the hall. The last thing she wanted to see was his hair, damp from the shower. She didn't want to smell the scent of soap, and she didn't want to consider that he could have used the same bar that she had to lather his chest, his middle…. Thoughts like that caused a tension in her she couldn't begin to dismiss.

She was also painfully aware that she wouldn't take the bus this week, that she would ride with him in his sporty little car to the employee parking lot—and then they would go their separate ways. She'd gone to her closet to pull out her favorite skirt and low-heeled shoes—and looked directly at the baby-blue skirt and sweater set Brett claimed was the perfect office outfit. She didn't think twice. Impulsively sweeping it off the hanger, she slipped it on. She kicked her everyday shoes to the back of the closet and stepped into her new pumps.

Brett was waiting at the door of the apartment for her, car keys in hand. They jangled as his hand imperceptibly dropped. So did his gaze. From the fuzzy round neckline of her sweater right down to the toes of her leather pumps.

"You're not going to work in that, are you?" he asked, obviously surprised she'd chosen to wear one of the new outfits they'd selected.

She ran a hand down the middle of her sweater, brushing at a nonexistent piece of lint. "You said it was the perfect office outfit. And I—I thought I should sort of…ease into this new wardrobe thing. So I didn't alarm everyone at work. They might wonder if I was breaking out of my beige shell or something."

"I see. Well. You look very nice."

Sunny self-consciously blushed. She didn't want him to think she was dressing up to impress him. "I do have a meeting, and I thought…well, you know." She let the explanation trail off. "Anyway, you picked it out."

He winked at her. "Ah, yes. Remind me that I have very good taste. And for your information, that good taste comes from my mother's side of the family."

Sunny briskly gathered her purse and purposely reached for her old coat. As if he knew exactly what she was doing, Brett grinned. But, thankfully, he said nothing.

The ride to Wintersoft was filled with two things: silence and trepidation. Sunny worried if anyone would notice that they were riding together. If so, she intended to make light of it. Carpooling, she'd say. It made sense.

Yet she knew Anna, in marketing, would corner her and want to know how she'd managed to get Brett alone. If only Anna knew how alone they'd been…

They'd shared an intimate weekend of breakfasts and lunches and dinners. She'd witnessed the way he sipped wine. She'd listened to him shower. She'd watched his eyes grow heavy at midnight. She'd slipped between the expensive sheets he'd purchased, and put her head on his pillows. She'd felt his lips move over hers. In her dreams and in her mind.

Sunny unconsciously shook her head.

"Yes?"

Startled, Sunny looked over at Brett, half-afraid he could read the thoughts that were running through her head.

"I was thinking about this weekend," she said automatically. "And...and how I neglected my work," she quickly revised.

Brett wheeled into the parking lot. "You usually work weekends?" He pulled into his assigned parking space. As a senior vice president of Wintersoft, he parked at the front of the lot. She'd forgotten that.

"I try to stay on top of things."

"Oh, yes. Little Miss Efficiency." He snapped the ignition switch off and pulled the keys free, tossing them in one swift move to the palm of his hand. "Probably working for a raise, huh?"

"Is that so bad?"

"No. I just wondered." His grin was lopsided. "Because work's the only thing we didn't talk about this weekend."

Reed Connors, vice president of global marketing, had just pulled up beside them. He stopped to knock on Brett's window, the perpetual smile he was known for on his handsome face. "Hey, you two," he said after Brett rolled down the window, "what's up?"

"Not much. And you?" Brett answered.

Reed's gaze strayed to Sunny, then slid back to Brett. She saw the unasked question in his dark eyes. "Brett says talking about work in the carpool is off-limits," she improvised quickly. "But, hey, I've got a meeting on my mind."

"Oh, you're carpooling now?"

"Just for a few weeks," Brett said. "It made sense.

Since we found out we live in the same apartment complex."

"Nice perk, Brett." Reed winked conspiratorially. Then he offered Sunny a sympathetic look. "He who drives gets to pick the radio station and set the rules. Even about work. That's why they call it the driver's seat."

"Then I may have to go back to taking the bus," she declared.

Both men laughed, and Reed rapped his knuckles across the window frame before taking off.

Sunny slumped against the seat. "You know what he was thinking?"

"Doesn't matter." Brett shrugged.

"Still, we don't want this to negatively impact our work. And I think it's going to. I think it's inevitable." She hitched the strap of her bag over her shoulder and reached for the door handle, then swiveled on the seat to step out.

"Wait, Sunny," he ordered.

She looked over her shoulder, one foot poised on the pavement. Brett's eyes were fastened on the hem of her skirt. Either that or the curve of her leg. Sunny froze, but her mind went into fast-forward and she uttered the first thing that went sailing through her mind. "You aren't going to do that 'shall we see if we find each other insufferable' thing in the employee parking lot, are you?"

He snorted. "A thread," he explained. "You've got a thread hanging from your skirt." He reached over and slipped one finger between it and her nylons. A prickle of sensation rushed over her nerve endings, leaving her breathless.

He snapped the thread in one deft movement, then handed it to her. "Now you'll be positively flawless—at your meeting."

Overhead, on the second floor, Emily Winters gazed out Carmella's window. Brett Hamilton always parked his car right beneath her office. ''Carmella…look! It appears Brett and Sunny have reached some kind of an understanding. Why, if my eyes aren't deceiving me, he just put his hand on her knee.''

Chapter Six

Brett gazed at his new roommate. Sunny was a sight. Sprawled in his leather chair, her wool skirt bunched up around her knees, her pumps kicked off and her eyes closed, she managed one pitiful groan and fell silent. "My feet are killing me," she finally muttered. "Of all days to make me the fetch and carry girl, it would have to be when I'm breaking in a new pair of shoes."

Brett responded in the most instinctive, primal way. He pulled up the leather ottoman, sat on it and scooped up one of Sunny's feet. Before she could tense, he started massaging her heel and the curve of her instep, his palm cupping the fine bones of her arch.

"Oh, that feels *so* good."

He grinned and kept kneading. "I overheard Dale Conrad in sales say you really had a nice sway on those heels."

Her right eye popped open. "Sway? He said 'sway'?" She sighed, and the eyelid drifted closed. "The old lech. The man's sixty if he's a day."

"A man's never too old to notice, Sunny." The pressure

Brett used imperceptibly increased. He wanted to get her attention. "*I* noticed," he drawled.

Both of Sunny's eyes popped open. "Noticed what?"

He bit back a smile. "That blue is a particularly charming color on you." He put her foot down and reached for the other. "It lends a little softness to that prim and proper edge."

"Forget that. The last thing a woman in the legal department wants to be is soft."

"Not soft in a negative way. Soft, in a confident way," he assured her. Sunny went still as their eyes caught and held. He didn't back down, not from what he saw in the surprised depths of her gaze. The woman did not always know how to accept a compliment, not on a personal level.

His forefinger tickled the side of her foot, then he wiggled her little toe, mostly to break the mounting tension that was growing between them. "I feel guilty. About buying you the pumps," he confessed.

"Don't. I chose to wear them."

He experimentally dragged his knuckles along the underside of her foot, but she didn't flinch or pull away. "But I don't want to make you miserable."

"You didn't. I should have known better than to wear them all day. My vanity got the best of me. I wanted to make this outfit look good."

"It did. Because of *you*." He watched in fascination as Sunny's jaw dropped slightly, as if she couldn't believe he was offering her another compliment.

"I—I didn't use very good judgment."

He feigned concern and picked up both of her feet, resting them on his knees as he massaged. "We aren't having a lapse in your cognitive powers, are we?"

"Only around you," she retorted. "And all these ridiculous demands you're making of me."

His hands, in identical motions, moved over her stockinged feet. "I've another."

"What?"

"I'm going to the pool to work out. Come with me. If nothing else—" he tweaked her toes "—you can soak your feet in the spa."

"I'm not *that* bad."

"Good. Come along, then." He dropped her feet so that her heels rested on the ottoman between the V of his legs, and skimmed her with an expectant look. For some strange reason he didn't want her to say no. He'd spent the entire day looking up and down the halls for her. He'd gotten rather used to having her around, and as much as he hated to admit it, he liked it. She didn't badger him with all that fake, flirtatious stuff, didn't manipulate men, conversations or compliments. "Dinner afterward," he wheedled.

Sunny hesitated, pulling her knees up, then wedging her arches against the side of the ottoman. A weary sigh rippled through her. "Oh, all right. Only because I'm so worn-out with all that running around today." She levered her shoulders off the chair and swung her feet to the floor. "But no surprises. Not today. Not for me."

The pool house was silent and empty, save for the *whomp-whomp-whomp* Brett made as he ran on the jogging machine. Not knowing how long this exercise regimen would take, Sunny hitched up the hems of her khaki pants, sat on a towel at the edge of the Jacuzzi, plunged her feet in the hot water and waited.

Through the mirrored wall she watched him. The sleeves were hacked off his T-shirt, and his biceps bulged as he ran. The cords in his neck were taut, and his chest heaved and swelled, pushing forward as if he were ready to cross some imaginary finish line. His belly was concave, and every once in a while, his T-shirt would lift as he ran, and expose a triangle of smooth flesh above his hip.

The ragged pair of cutoff sweats hit him midthigh. His legs were deeply tanned and covered with coarse, curling hair. His thighs were solid, and his calves tapered down to thick ankles. Every part of him came together in a fluid, graceful way—the long, striated muscles, the thick bones. A damp sheen glistened on his shoulders and arms, and without breaking stride, he tossed a white hand towel around his neck.

The strangest feeling fluttered through Sunny's middle. It was as if she were privy to one of Brett's private moments, when he pushed himself, tested himself. Her heart did a little flip-flop. Then she straightened and looked away, to organize her thoughts and recover her temporary loss of control.

The biggest surprise of the evening was that Brett ran five miles three times a week, Sunny decided. And then her parents walked in the door.

She yanked her feet out of the Jacuzzi and hurriedly dried them.

"Sunshine!" her father called, waving. "What are you doing here?"

"Oh, just...taking advantage of the services." Sunny grabbed her sandals.

"So are we!" her mother exclaimed, quickly walking across the room. Her hair floated in wild disarray over a bright flowered muumuu as she bent to give Sunny a hug. "Guess what? Your father's arranged to use the community room to start a meditation group. Isn't that wonderful? And if things work out, we may get a food co-op going here on Saturday mornings."

"Oh. Wow." Behind her Sunny heard the jogging machine start to slow. *Wah-whomp, wah-whomp.* Apprehension washed through her, but she didn't dare turn around.

"We're gonna meditate and gravitate, right to the center of our universe," her father acknowledged happily, smoothing the front of his tie-dyed T-shirt. "Every Monday and Wednesday, from seven to nine."

"But...what happened with the candles and the soap— and the place in Vermont?"

"In time." Her father nodded.

"When opportunities present themselves, you have to

take them,'' her mother agreed philosophically. Sunny had
an inkling her parents were getting far too comfortable. The
alarming thought went zooming through her head that she
might *never* get them out of her apartment. ''And how are
you getting along, honey?''

''Oh, fine.''

Her mother waited for her to say more, and when she
didn't, proudly added, ''I did a huge batch of soap yesterday. Remind me to give you some. We labeled it and tied
it with raffia. Oatmeal and honey. And the co-op said
they'd take as much as they could get. Your living room
is a real assembly line right now.''

Sunny's eyelids went half-mast and her shoulders grew
taut, as she imagined the mess.

''I'm afraid, Sunshine, that your mother may turn into
one of those manufacturing zealots that spouts Republican-
ism and pays itinerants under the table. If she wasn't bar-
tering that soap with the food co-op, I'd be concerned.''

''So,'' Sunny said slowly as the realization hit. ''This
sounds like you're going to stay longer than you thought.''

Her father and mother exchanged glances. ''You know,
we're kind of settling in,'' he admitted. ''It's the strangest
thing. I never thought I'd feel that way about Boston.''

''But it's still my apartment,'' Sunny reminded them.
''I'll still be moving back in.''

''Of course, of course,'' her mother said. ''And we want
you to. But—'' her smile widened ''—how's the boyfriend?'' she asked slyly.

The jogging machine ground to a halt.

''He's not my boyfriend,'' Sunny said, planting her feet
and making sure her back was squarely to Brett. ''We're
just friends.''

''It doesn't matter what you call it these days,'' her father said patiently, ''it's still the same thing. You live with
somebody and get in touch with your feelings and—''

''We're not in touch!'' Sunny insisted. ''We're not even
on the same wavelength! We don't have anything in com-

mon. He's from England, I'm from all over. He plays tennis, and I grew up thinking tennis rackets were for chasing bats out of old houses. He went to private schools and I didn't even get to go to public schools—''

"Home-schooling is a privilege," her father reminded her.

"Hello," Brett interrupted, coming to stand at Sunny's shoulder. "I'm Brett Hamilton." He extended his to hand her father. "I suspect you must be Sylvia and Doug."

Her mother brightened. "This is the man you're living with, Sunny?"

"I'm *not* living with him!"

"Right now we're saying we're roommates," he stated calmly.

The twenty-five bracelets her mother typically wore on her wrist jangled against each other as she clasped Brett's hand. "That's good enough for me," she assured him.

"I don't have to tell you we're real happy about this, son," her father confided. "Sharing living space is an integral part of communing with society. It's basic human nature, and there's nothing shameful about it. Why, back in my day and age, love-ins and live-ins were the happening thing. No one made excuses and no one thought much about it."

Sunny fervently wished the floor would simply open up and swallow her whole. As it was she had to settle for her eyes rolling back in her head. "Sylvia. Doug. Listen to me. This is a perfectly platonic relationship."

"It was," Brett solemnly agreed. "Until we messed it up with that kiss."

Hearing the revelation, Sunny jumped as if she'd been shot. Then she swiveled and glared up at Brett.

"That's a start, that's a start," her father said encouragingly.

Brett cleared his throat noisily. His face was tight, as if he was trying to bite back a grin. "Now, we're, um, *appreciating* what we can each bring to the relationship."

Sunny could actually hear the smile in his voice, and for some reason it took the edge off the indignation she felt. He was an outrageous tease.

"Well, we know what Sunny can bring to a relationship," her mother said proudly. "But what about you, Brett?" Before he had time to reply, she said, "Say, have you kids eaten? Come back to Sunny's apartment. I'll fix dinner and we can talk."

"Sounds good to me," Brett answered. "We were going to a restaurant, but we could skip that." Then, turning to Sunny, he solicitously draped an arm around her shoulders. "Is that okay with you, luv? I'd like to get to know your parents. And you've had a hard day. You should sit back and put your feet up."

"Brett, you aren't going to find a lot of red meat at my apartment," she warned.

"I'll fix pancakes," her mother offered. "Everybody loves pancakes!"

"Oh, ho, ho," Doug chortled, looking inordinately pleased. "My old lady makes a mean zucchini pancake!"

"Zucchini?"

"Squash," Sunny said flatly. "It's a vegetable you can add to anything."

"Zucchini pancakes and homemade maple syrup. And that syrup's imported." Her father winked. "From Vermont. Doesn't get much better than that."

Three pairs of eyes turned expectantly to Sunny. She had no choice; she was cornered. Brett lazily cocked his head to one side, waiting for her answer. He'd baited her into going, and she knew it. But the way his fingers plucked at her sleeve unknowingly raised goose bumps beneath the fabric. The way his sea-blue eyes mocked her turned her inside out.

She fought the arousing sensations he provoked, refused to look too deeply into the beckoning light of his eyes. Refused to submit to the yearning that curled in her middle.

"Actually, I think it sounds like a great idea," she said. "Then we'll all get a little taste of something new."

Sunny had forgotten that her mother had mentioned she'd made soap. The apartment smelled like oatmeal cookies, and the faint aroma of the vanilla candles still lingered. The place smelled wonderful—but it looked like a wreck.

Her furniture had been rearranged, and the sedate linen-covered sofa and matching chair was piled high with shoe boxes filled with soap. Bits of raffia littered the floor. Her glass-topped coffee table was spattered with candle wax and a dozen half-burned votives.

To her horror, her mother had hung curtains of plastic beads over several doorways, including the one to the galley kitchen. Sunny was drawn to the red plastic beads like a moth to a flame.

"Mom, why did you put these up?"

"Oh, they add a nice touch, don't you think? Kind of cheer the place up a little. And every time you walk in and out it's like having music all around you."

"But I don't like that kind of music," she said, unable to keep the plea out of her voice. Swiping the strands of beads back with her palm, Sunny surveyed the kitchen in stunned silence. The soap-making mess compounded the candle-making one. She let the curtain of beads fall back into place. "Of course, the nice thing about them is they are a screen." She turned and blocked the doorway so that Brett couldn't see the chaos. She didn't want him to realize that his dinner was coming out of the throes of hell. "Sit down, sit down," she urged. "I'll help Mom. I know where everything is."

Brett glanced uneasily at the sofa and chair. "I can't. They're, um, occupied."

"I'll get that, I'll get that," her father offered, picking up a stack of shoe boxes and setting them out of the way, in a corner. He offered Brett a cigarette lighter. "Go ahead,'' he indicated, nodding to the candle stubs on the coffee table. ''We've got candles to burn.''

''Is that what smells so good in here?''

Her father shrugged and turned his attention to cleaning off the chair. ''I'm partial to incense myself. But Sylvia says it reminds her of organized religion.''

Brett lifted an amused eyebrow and systematically lit every candle on the table.

For the next half hour, Sunny felt disjointed and uncomfortable, as if she was all body parts. She listened with one ear while she set the table with one hand and picked up with the other. She hurried to right the mess, kicking stuff out of the way and bumping doors closed with her hip.

Her father, who kept a cursory conversation going with Brett, was on good behavior. Her mother, who had managed to ruin every last pan in Sunny's kitchen, happily stood at the counter and pulled ingredients out of the cupboards.

By the time dinner was ready, Sunny would have eaten a stack of cardboard slathered in Wite-Out. She didn't know why it meant so much but she wanted her parents to present a normal enough image to be likable. Brett was used to formal and customary; her parents were anything but.

She and Brett had come from different ends of the spectrum, on everything from politics to religion. He had been raised with tradition; she had been raised as a nonconformist.

If opposites were ever to attract, she and Brett would be the most likely candidates.

''These are good!'' he exclaimed, forking up a second bite.

''It's the syrup,'' her father explained. ''All natural.''

''I've made these pancakes for years,'' Sylvia said. ''But with the maple syrup we tapped in Vermont...'' She left the rest unsaid.

''We want to buy a little place in Vermont,'' Sunny's

father confided. "Tap sugar maples. Live off the land. We'll make a little money with these natural recipe products. People are into that, you know. They are ready to go back to the basics."

"I can't believe it." Brett looked over at Sunny. "You ate like this all the time?"

"That, stir-fry and a lot of tofu."

"We tried harvesting sea kelp when we were in Texas, but we didn't have much luck at it." Her father shrugged as if it had been a multimillion-dollar investment that had gone sour.

"Or the bean sprouts we tried to raise in California," her mother added.

"You did have a nice herb garden in Washington state, though," her father said between mouthfuls.

Brett's fork paused in midair. "Sunny? You've lived in all those places?"

"Those and a lot more," her father confirmed expansively. "Just like that song. You and me and a dog named Boo. We set out to see the country and we did. We saw it from every back road and every old man's perspective. We saw it from the back of a pickup and the back of a VW bus. We've always said we're going to write a book. I figure when we get settled in Vermont we'll get it all on paper. When it's finished, Sunny's going to have quite a legacy."

Brett poured more syrup on his pancakes. "It sounds like you've already provided her with quite an interesting life."

"More than you want to know, Brett," she said, impulsively laying her hand on his forearm. "More than you can possibly imagine."

He covered her hand with his, sandwiching it with his warmth. His knuckles grazed her skin and his fingers curled over hers, the blunt-cut fingernails gently scraping her flesh. The gesture was possessive and poignant and private—and her parents didn't miss it. "I want you tell me about it," he said softly. "All of it."

Sunny stared at him, momentarily convinced he meant it, that he didn't judge her unconventional upbringing. But of course he didn't mean it, her rational side reminded her.

This was a man who had traveled all over the world. He'd skied the French Alps. He'd sailed the Mediterranean and snorkeled in the Caribbean. He'd stayed at five-star hotels where bellhops carried his luggage. He'd called room service when he was hungry. He'd never eaten strawberries out of an open field or carried all his belongings in a knapsack or camped in a tent in the rain.

No, they were worlds apart, Sunny reminded herself. She shouldn't be feeling the way she was…because it would never last. Certainly not any longer than it took his parents to get back on the plane bound for England.

She tensed, ready to jerk her hand free…but she couldn't bring herself to do it. She saw genuine curiosity in Brett's features, and it endeared him to her all the more. "Sometime," she said, in an equally soft tone. "Sometime I'll tell you all about our journey."

Chapter Seven

No sooner had Sunny started to slip into the perfectly rational, wonderfully routine world of Brett Hamilton than she realized his parents really were coming to visit. Everything was destined to change. In a heartbeat.

The moment the analogy went through her head, she loathed and regretted it. For everything about her heart was out of control. Brett Hamilton pulled at her heartstrings; he gave new meaning to the word *heartthrob*. They'd had heart-to-heart talks; they'd shared heartwarming moments and heart-rending arguments.

The man was a blackguard. A vile, insensitive, unfeeling jerk. How *could* he do this to her?

How could she possibly pretend to be in love with him and not feel something? He brushed against her as they passed in the hall, and her senses sailed into hyperdrive. He helped her with her coat, and she ached to feel his fingers smooth her hair away from her collar or against her neck. He took sharp turns in the car and called them "opportunity corners," grinning wickedly when her shoulder thudded against his.

They were supposed to be engaged, and lately, whenever he elicited all these strange and exciting feelings, she looked at her empty fourth finger, left hand, and wondered. She simply wondered.

What would it be like to be paired with this man for an eternity? What would it be like to share her darkest secrets, to explore the mysteries of intimacy? With him. With a man who made her heart tremble and her pulse quicken?

It had gotten to the point where she couldn't stand looking at the void on her hand, and she couldn't bear considering the charade. His parents would expect something visible, so she did the most natural thing in the world: she went to a department store and bought herself an engagement ring. She had to wear it; she might as well like how it looked.

It was their last night alone together, without his parents. Somehow, to Sunny, that seemed significant. They had just walked in the door from work. Brett, with his coat still on, sorted his mail.

Taking a deep breath, Sunny let her hand float in midair, between them. "What do you think?" she asked.

"About what?" he said absently, studying an advertisement.

"This." Her hand trembled. "I'm trying to be convincing."

Brett tossed the mail aside, then turned back. His expression froze and he stared, fixing his gaze on the single round stone, the silver setting. "Hey. You're…engaged."

For several seconds, neither of them spoke. But Sunny's heart hammered in her chest and she held her breath. Awareness intensified, prickling her nerve endings.

"To me," he said finally, quietly.

"If you don't like it—"

"No, I…" He reached out to snag her fingers and look, really look, at the stone, the setting. He turned her finger so that the ring refracted the light. "Where did you get this, anyway?"

"That discount store over on Larch."

Brett paused. "It's…shiny." Then his lower lip wiggled and his chin wobbled. He ducked his head. "I hope it won't turn your finger green."

Sunny jerked her hand back. "I'm trying to be helpful here."

"I see that." Brett gave in to the impulse and let his grin widen.

"And you make some scathing comment—"

"Now hold on…" Brett laid a hand on her arm, astonished to find Sunny was shaking. God, he didn't want to hurt her feelings—but his mother would take one look at that ring and yelp. The woman knew color, clarity and carats as intimately as Sunny's parents knew zucchini. She talked about cuts as if she were in the meat department. "If it was up to me—" he shrugged "—I'd say the ring would do. But it's my mother I'm thinking about, Sunny. The woman has the uncanny ability to recognize a paste stone from fifty yards."

"So we tell her it's temporary. Which it is, of course, so we wouldn't be lying or—"

"I've got a better idea." He squeezed her arm and felt an insane pleasure at the small intimacy. "Let's replace it with something genuine."

"A real ring? A diamond ring?"

The disbelief in Sunny's voice undermined him. Brett gazed at the dismal little ring she'd chosen, and experienced a nagging desire to make things right. She deserved more than that—even if it was all a farce. "Real enough to be convincing," he grumbled, suddenly disgruntled with all the turbulence this so-called engagement was causing him.

Window-shopping this time around had implications. Deeper implications.

"Let's just go in and get something," Brett said finally. Sunny stood rooted to the spot, her eyes glued on the embossed plastic price tags. "Do you think they'll let us bring it back?" she whispered.

"This isn't a refrigerator."

She said nothing, then pointed to a ring in the corner. "That's the cheapest one. And it costs four times more than a refrigerator."

"Sunny!" he said in exasperation. "This isn't anything functional, it's…"

"What?"

"It's a promise—and sometimes promises cost like bloody hell."

He was angry about more than the engagement ring, she realized. "I don't think I can do this."

"We'll do it together," he said stoically.

"It costs so much money. And the stone may be genuine, but the promises aren't, and—"

"And don't say any more, will you?" he implored, running a hand through his hair. "I don't care what it costs. It's the end result that matters. I've come this far and I'm not backing down now."

"Do you want to hear my argument again, about how we can tell your parents we're going to pick out a ring later? That this is just something to get by with?"

"No."

Sunny stalled, considering. "I suppose you can hock it afterward."

"I won't *want* the bloody ring. You can have it reset or something. Use it as a cocktail ring."

"I don't do cocktails. You know that."

"Sunny…" He moved away from the window and opened the door to the jeweler's. "I don't care what you do with the ring after we break up. Let's just get engaged— and let's do it now. I insist."

A woman exiting the store gave Brett the strangest look.

Sunny couldn't resist; the moment was priceless. "Well, I guess. If you insist…darling," she answered, loud enough so the woman heard.

Brett heaved a sigh and shut his eyes briefly. "Nice touch. But do you know," he said, still holding the door ajar, "that this is the first time I've really experienced your sense of humor? And, unfortunately, it has to be at my expense."

"Literally? Or figuratively?"

"Gauging from the price of those diamonds, both."

The skinny, twenty-something salesman behind the counter, James, was effusive with his congratulations and engaging in his chatter about diamonds and settings. Brett and Sunny listened politely. James compared quality; he talked about the cut. He urged Sunny to try on an exquisite wedding set, just to test the weight. Her insistence that they were only looking for something small and simple fell on deaf ears, and Sunny reluctantly tried the ring he suggested on her finger.

Something changed in that moment. The diamond, flashing blue fire, became a scintillating orb of energy. It drew them together, Brett's shoulder settling against hers, the heat of his body igniting hers as they gazed together into the mesmerizing depths.

Like a crystal ball, Sunny thought inanely, this ring predicted their future.

Just that quickly, the diamond winked at her.

Just that quickly!

The room started spinning, and James's voice faded to background music. Colors collided and meshed, smells became more intense. The scent of Brett's leather coat teased her nostrils; the lingering scent of his aftershave heightened her awareness. His hand, in a kind of disjointed animation, reached for hers, to turn the ring beneath the lights, and he was so warm.... The coarse hair on the back of his hand was so dramatically different than the taut fine skin stretching across hers. His fingers were broad and thick, hers long and tapered. And yet they seemed to fit. So well. Agonizingly well.

The blue veins beneath his knuckles throbbed with a life

only she seemed to recognize. His wrists were solid and strong, and the second hand of his watch—an expensive little platinum number—ticked resolutely forward. Perhaps to some preordained destiny.

With all the forces coming together into a cataclysmic clash, Sunny lost herself...to the charade, and to Brett's captivating appeal. She knew she'd never get all of herself back, and she didn't even care.

"It's a bit too heavy for your finger," she heard James announce. He peeled it off and placed a dazzling tray of rings at their fingertips instead.

"That's pretty," Sunny heard herself say.

"Look at that." Brett pointed to one set with a sapphire.

"Mmm...try this," James plucked a ring out of the tray and started to reach for her finger, then stopped—and offered it to Brett instead. The round diamond was modest, and seemed to float above two smaller stones, one on each side.

Accepting the token without pause, Brett captured her fingers and slowly edged it on, over the tip of her nail, over her nail bed and cuticle, and over the first knuckle. With firm pressure he wiggled it over her second knuckle, and the significance of the gesture inflamed Sunny's desire, enhanced her senses.

"It's perfect," he said triumphantly, lifting her knuckle to roll her finger under the fluorescent lights.

It was. Perfect in every way.

"I..."

"Nice color, a flawless stone. The baguettes on each side of the center stone make it distinctive," James commented.

"I like it," Brett said.

"It's larger than we planned to get."

"It's an investment," James pointed out.

Hearing the words, both Brett and Sunny swiveled to face him. It was an investment in Brett's future. Hadn't he said that himself?

It also brought the illusion crashing down. Reality was only a heartbeat away.

"We'll take it," Brett said stiffly, pulling a credit card out of his wallet.

"Oh, no." Sunny started to yank the ring off her finger, determined that she wouldn't be saddled with this ring, with these expectations. " A simple solitaire, that's all."

Brett stopped her, curling his fingers around hers, his palm over the back of her hand. "It's you," he said softly. "It's perfect."

Looking up, Sunny caught Brett's blue gaze. His words tumbled through her head. *It's you. It's perfect.* The fleeting seconds became imprinted on her memory, and she knew, intrinsically, that they would never be erased. His voice echoed, and in the deepest chambers of her mind she could replay the resonance, the inflection of his voice—right down to the way his tongue touched the roof of his mouth as he slowly bit off the last syllable.

She debated miserably about what she should do.

"It's not too high a price to pay," he insisted. "Trust me."

Trust him? Oh, God, she wanted to. She wanted to trust him, and believe him, and wish for the slightest while that this would all last, that it would never go away.

Sunny wavered. "I..."

"Will say yes," Brett finished for her.

Slowly, decisively, she closed her mouth over the objection. Brett, his gaze still fastened on hers, deliberately released her hand and offered the credit card to James.

Accepting the card and filling out the paperwork, James smiled like a sage. "This is the kind of ring that lasts a lifetime," he said. "Congratulations. I can see that you're going to be very happy together."

Having a complete stranger foretell their future was like another dash of cold water. Both Brett and Sunny looked away guiltily.

She fiddled with the ring, straightening it on her finger.

Brett fixed his attention on a display of pearl necklaces. "Do you have pearls?" he asked abruptly. Sunny followed his gaze.

"I have these…." She made a flapping gesture near her chest.

"Imitations."

"Faux," she stated.

"Faux pas," he retorted. "To wear something like that around my mother. No. We need something classic for you to wear to dinner with my parents. They'll approve."

James put the paperwork aside and quickly opened the case and displayed four strands for their inspection. Brett didn't wait for Sunny to argue or exclaim over them. He chose a strand and picked it up, unclasping it. Carefully, he lifted the pearls over Sunny's head and draped them over her sweater.

The pads of his fingers brushed her nape. Her skin tingled, tiny vibrations radiating out across her shoulders and up into her scalp. To have him stand behind her in such close proximity made her conscious of details.

The creases in the sleeves of his jacket made a whispering sound, the creak of leather rubbing against leather. She heard the indistinct jangle of keys and pocket change as he shifted. Heard his breath, moving like a whisper over her bare skin.

If having Brett slip the ring on her finger was romantic, this gesture was purely seductive.

"I think," he said, pausing to work the clasp, "this is the right length."

The clasp caught and held, and, regretfully, Brett's hands fell away—only to settle on her shoulders. It was all Sunny could do to look in the mirror and admire the shimmering, opalescent pearls.

She visualized instead the virginal white of a wedding gown, with seed pearls scattering the bodice, a strand of pearls at her throat. Lifting her hand, she touched the pearls, and the diamond they had chosen snared her attention. Like a dream, a vision, it came to her. They were paired before the oval mirror and captured in a shard of time, like an engaged couple posing for their portrait.

The visage swept her breath away.

"And these," Brett announced, to no one in particular, "put the finishing touch on the illusion."

Sunny was a nervous wreck. She'd made a mess of every project she'd started that day. Her mind was elsewhere. On Brett. On the imminent meeting with his parents. On the ring she'd had to leave in the box, in the confines of a dresser drawer in the apartment.

She worried the silly ring would be gone when she got home. Maybe someone would break in to the apartment and steal it. Maybe she'd lose it, what with taking it off and putting it on all the time, as she'd need to do.

She walked around all day feeling as if she had a secret, one that was so big and so unreal that no one would believe it. She found herself staring at Mindy in accounting, and wondered what she would think if she knew Sunny was unofficially "engaged" to Brett Hamilton. Mindy had told her just last week she would just die—simply die—if Brett ever asked her out for dinner and drinks. Sunny couldn't possibly tell her they shared three meals a day—plus two bedrooms and one bath.

She worried about his parents. She couldn't imagine how she'd keep a conversation going—and didn't know if she could. Maybe she should just keep her mouth shut and smile a lot. For some insane reason she wanted his parents to like her, but it wouldn't matter one whit whether they did or not. For this was all for show. All of it, she reminded herself sternly.

Then there was Brett. He was uneasy, too. She could tell. He didn't talk as much, not as he had at first. He seemed suddenly uncomfortable about her, because he was making too much of a to-do about ensuring that she was comfortable. *Would you like something other than wine, Sunny? If you're cold, I can get you an extra blanket. Hold on, let me get that door, your hands are full.*

How could he possibly know she wanted to learn what it was like to share the same glass with him, to snuggle when she was chilled or walk over a threshold *with* him, not in front of him?

No, most likely he was just being polite. He was probably afraid she'd back out and leave him high and dry.

An hour before closing time, Emily stopped by her cubicle. "Sunny? You okay?"

Startled, she dropped the file she was holding. Papers scattered all over her desk, all over the floor. "I—I'm fine. Why? Don't I look okay?"

"Brett said—you know—today's the day."

"Oh. Yeah. That." Sunny ignored the mishmash of papers and made no move to pick them up. "Yes, today's the day I'm going to be discovered as a fraud and a cheat."

"C'mon. It's not that dire. Carmella says you're doing him a favor."

"Oh, how little you know." Sunny, who was not given to theatrics, suddenly felt like a drama queen.

"Not everything about Brett's *that* bad."

"Oh, no, everything about Brett is *good.* Incredibly good. Now I'm afraid I'll let him down. That something will go wrong and I'll say something stupid, or trip over my feet, or—"

Emily cocked her head, then stepped inside the office and closed the door. "Sunny, do you need a pep talk?" she asked solicitously.

"I don't think so. Brett's incredibly good at that, too." She let a second slip away, considering. "Frankly, I don't think there's anything the man isn't incredibly good at."

"Then what's wrong?"

"I misjudged him. He's a nice guy. Too nice. I'll be the first to say he shouldn't be cornered into marrying someone, and I'd do anything to help him stop it. But..."

"Yes?"

"I have this nagging thing going through the back of my head." Sunny picked up a few of the scattered papers and tried to look unaffected. "What if his folks don't like me?"

"Sunny! Why should you care? You could be Lady Dracula and he'd still pretend to be smitten with you!"

Sunny swallowed. There it was. The biggest, ugliest word in the English language: *pretend.* Somehow, starting this last week, Sunny wanted Brett to simply like her for herself. Not because he had to or was obligated to.

"God, Sunny, just wiggle under his arm and hold his hand, and kiss him, and—well, act like you're madly in love!"

"We're doing those things, anyway," Sunny muttered. She tossed the papers back on the desk.

"Excuse me?"

"For effect. For effect," Sunny clarified, raising her voice as she flapped her hand. She had no intention of explaining the whopper of a kiss Brett had pasted her with. Or the times he'd slung an affectionate arm around her shoulders, or grabbed her hand to show her something. Or the indefinable moment when he'd slipped a ring on her finger and pearls around her neck.

"Well, then. I suppose you wouldn't feel too uncomfortable being together for the dinner party Dad is having in a couple of weeks, would you? Brett's supposed to come, and I thought it would just make sense if he brought you. That's okay, isn't it?"

"Oh, sure. My future is out of my hands. But you better ask Brett. His folks might be gone by then."

"Why would that matter?"

"There won't be any point in keeping up the charade, would there?"

"Sunny, maybe by then the reason you'll be together is that you *choose* to be."

Chapter Eight

The plane was late. Brett and Sunny burned off their anxiety by walking and quizzing each other.

"My best friend was…?"

"John. John Chesterfield."

"I met him where?"

"Highfields Academy, where you both went to school. He was a year older than you and your mother blamed him for getting you into so much trouble."

"Precisely."

"Your father liked John until he invited him to go sailing with your family, and he accidentally set the boat adrift. It happened in July, the day before your mother's birthday."

Brett's stride faltered as he looked down at her. "You have an amazing memory," he praised.

"Don't worry, my mind will go blank the moment your parents walk down the gangplank."

"Runway," he automatically corrected.

"Whatever. Gangplank feels like the more appropriate term. I figure this debacle will either make me sink or swim."

"Sunny, don't you have any confidence in yourself?"

She worried the ring on her fourth finger, left hand. "Not particularly, no."

"My parents are going to love you!"

But apparently they didn't plan to love her. Not one little bit. For the moment they passed through the gate, and Sunny recognized the sour expression on her future mother-in-law's face, she wilted. Her father-in-law looked equally grim. Sunny's knees nearly buckled.

Brett stepped forward briskly. "Mother! Father!" he called, raising his arm the same way he'd hail a cab.

His mother swiveled, her chin lifted and her perfectly plucked eyebrows raised to an impossible degree. Her eyes were bright and sharp, and they briefly settled on Brett. Then her full, dark lashes narrowed to a discreet line as she gave Sunny the once-over.

To withstand the scrutiny, Sunny made her frozen mouth smile back.

The soft contours of Lady Miriam's features were strained. Brick-red lipstick outlined her pinched mouth, and a recent dusting of face powder put a matte finish on her pallor. Against her navy-blue traveling suit, her flashy gold and sapphire jewelry—bracelet, pendant and eardrops—made a singular upscale statement. The wide brim of her matching hat perched atop swirls of platinum-blond hair.

Had she met this woman in the mall or on the street, Sunny would have cut a wide swath around her.

Lord Arthur's features, however, relaxed the moment he laid eyes on his son. His sooty hair carried a glimmer of gray at the temples and was perfectly styled in the classic "businessman's cut." His cheeks, stained a slightly ruddy color, boasted the weathered look of sport. Sunny saw parts of Brett in his father's good looks—the broad forehead, blunt chin and strong jawline. He was robust and hearty, and wore a suit and tie as if they were casual clothes. He carried an umbrella in one hand, a newspaper in the other.

"Mother." Brett kissed her on the cheek, using obvious

care not to bump her hat or disturb her makeup. She patted him affectionately on the back and turned to Sunny, waiting for the introduction. ''Father.'' Brett's father embraced him with a bear hug, the paper crumpling, the umbrella jutting out at a dangerous angle.

''You're looking good, my boy.''

''I am,'' Brett agreed, his smile growing. ''And you can blame her for that. Darling, I'd like you to meet my parents. Lady Miriam and Lord Arthur Hamilton.''

Sunny extended her hand, and then instinct kicked in; she bobbed slightly, almost in a curtsy. ''Lady Hamilton, Lord Hamilton.''

''What is this?'' Brett chided. ''You aren't bobbing around like the day maid, are you?''

Sunny flushed. ''I'm just so pleased to finally meet your parents. You've spoken so highly of them.''

Lady Miriam withdrew her limp, lifeless hand from Sunny's and cast a suspicious eye on her son. Obviously she didn't believe a word of Sunny's nonsense.

Lord Hamilton jumped into the fray. ''My dear,'' he acknowledged, the obligatory pressure of his hand firm, not warm. ''We, on the other hand, know almost nothing about you.''

The simple sentence laid one truth bare: they were there to find out.

''Then we'll have a lot to talk about, won't we?'' Sunny replied, forcing a lighthearted note into her words that she certainly didn't feel.

''More than you can possibly know,'' Lady Hamilton said without a hint of kindness. ''And your name is, again?''

''Sunny,'' Brett stated, circling her waist with a possessive squeeze. ''Sunny Robbins.''

''Sonny? A…'' his mother gazed at her in undisguised horror ''…*boy's* name?''

''Oh, no,'' Sunny said quickly, ''Sunny as in—Sunshine.'' It was too late to call the words back, but she wanted to, desperately. Brett's mother didn't change expression; his father lifted his eyebrows. "My parents said I was the sunshine of their lives. They are rather sentimental about…things."

"My. How…fascinating."

Sunny knew Lady Hamilton thought it was anything but.

"A clever, informal little nickname." Lord Hamilton tried to smile, but Sunny realized the effort pained him.

"Actually," she said, experiencing a perverse twinge of pleasure, "it's my real name. Sunshine Nirvana Robbins."

A small moan escaped Lady Hamilton, and she pressed the back of her hand to her mouth. Her eyes shuttered as if she were going to swoon.

"Mother!"

"I—I was just thinking, my dear." Her hand settled on Brett's sleeve, as if to steady herself. "How your names would look on the wedding announcements. There are a lot of—" she lifted her shoulders as if she were at a loss for words "—letters."

"Don't worry. We haven't set a date yet, Mother."

"That's good news," his father replied encouragingly.

"Then it won't be soon?"

Sunny detected the hopeful note in Lady Hamilton's voice, and for an instant was genuinely grateful that she would never actually be engaged to or marry Brett. The baggage he carried with him was almost as daunting as hers.

"Mother, let's get you settled at your hotel," Brett soothed, changing the subject. "We've got a week to tell you about all our plans, and it's late, and I know you want to get unpacked and settled."

Lady Hamilton, barely distracted, nodded, then said, "I see she has a ring."

Sunny felt as if she weren't even there, yet her hand popped up as if it had a will of its own. "We picked it out together," she said boldly, convinced that she was indeed doing the right thing.

Lady Hamilton stared at it, and not a shred of emotion crossed her face. "It's a nice, simple little setting," she finally allowed. "Certainly not ostentatious."

His father harrumphed. "Affordable. Under the circumstances," he agreed.

Even to Sunny's untrained ears the implication was clear: Brett's inheritance hung in the balance. She looked over at him, worry pricking her consciousness. He appeared unaffected, unruffled.

"Are you hungry?" he asked. "If so, we can find a nice restaurant."

"No, no." Lady Hamilton waved away the offer. "I'd rather check into the hotel and start the day off fresh tomorrow. Things always look brighter in the morning, and I'd like my first impression of—" she stopped abruptly, skimming an embarrassed look over Sunny "—Boston...yes, Boston," she clarified, "to be the best."

"My parents have never been here," Brett explained, keeping his arm firmly around Sunny. "So this is a first. For everything, including my engagement."

"We usually go to New York," Lord Hamilton said. "Or Florida. I must say I do like that tropical climate."

They made small talk at the carousel while they waited for their bags. When everything was in order, Brett ushered them to a waiting cab and mentioned that they'd be relying on cabs for their visit, as he had purchased a small sports car. The hotel was only minutes from Brett's apartment, and during the forty minute cab ride they talked about Brett's transition to living in America, and the responsibilities of his job. They were nice, safe topics, all of them.

Everyone piled out at the hotel to say good-night, even Sunny. As Brett helped haul out their bags and put them on the curb for the bellboy, his father came out of the lobby flapping a sheet of paper. "Our reservations are in a bit of a muddle," he announced. "And the manager says there's not a room to be had, not on this side of town. Something about a Celtics exhibition game? And a handbell festival?"

"And there's the Patriots game, too." Brett paused, suitcase in hand. "I didn't think of that."

"It's almost eleven o'clock at night," Sunny reminded him, checking her watch. "Should we call around?"

"I don't know. I don't have a backup plan. We could take them farther out of town, but the accommodations might not be as nice…and it will be quite a drive."

The four of them shifted uncomfortably.

Lady Hamilton looked puzzled. "Brett? I thought you said you had a two-bedroom apartment."

"I do. But—"

"We'll just stay with you, dear," she announced, as if the matter were settled.

Sunny paled, suddenly grateful that the parking lot lights were dim.

"Mother. Father…" Brett, obviously at a loss for words, hesitated. He covered by putting the suitcase back in the taxi. "I'm not sure you'd be comfortable at my place."

"And I have my things scattered all over the second bedroom," Sunny interjected quickly.

"It doesn't matter. It's not like you're using the bed in the second bedroom, are you?"

Sunny gasped for air, then swallowed uncomfortably. That *was* the premise; they were supposed to be living with each other, on every intimate level.

Brett buzzed her temple with a kiss. "We can give Mother and Father the extra bedroom, can't we, darling? I can't imagine them on a blow-up mattress in the middle of the living room floor, can you?"

The idea of Lord and Lady Hamilton rolling around on an inflatable bed did stir her imagination. Forcing a smile and steeling her already jangled nerves, Sunny shook her head. "Absolutely not. I'll move a few of my things out of the closet. To make sure you have enough space," she told Brett's mother. "We want you to be comfortable while you're here."

"Thank you," Lady Miriam said, a trace of benevolence tinting her reply.

"You know," Sunny offered brightly, a vision of her knocking on the door of her own apartment at midnight tumbling through her head, "maybe I could stay with a friend. Or something."

"No, no, no," Brett insisted, pulling her close against his side. "I want Mother and Father to get to know you...and how can they do that if you're somewhere else?" His smile was firm, and determination hardened his eyes. "Besides, it will be so cozy to be together like this. Much nicer than a hotel. Don't you think, luv?"

Sunny had no choice but to agree. "If that's what you want...darling."

"Fine." Lady Hamilton waved her hand dismissively. "We're off to your place. For the duration."

Brett followed Sunny into the extra bedroom. "Here," he offered, "let me help you carry your things into my bedroom."

"If you think for one minute," she whispered, "that I'm sleeping with you—"

"I don't think—" he grabbed a batch of her clothes by the hangers and draped them over his arm "—that you're going to do anything *more* than sleep with me, that's all."

"In the same bed? Forget it."

"Well, that's how this living together thing usually works. And we're doing it, you know. Or at least we're *supposed* to be *doing it*. Living together, I mean."

Given his poor choice of words, she took a deep breath. "Brett, I'm doing you a favor, but—"

"Here, let me help, son." His father stood in the doorway, his curious gaze sliding from Brett to Sunny and back again.

She snapped her mouth closed and haphazardly stuffed the remains of her underwear into a canvas tote. Brett offered his father the clothes he carried. When Lord Arthur disappeared, heading toward Brett's bedroom, Brett walked over to Sunny and stood behind her.

"About that favor…" he began, his hands settling on her shoulders. "I'll make sure you're comfortable."

She turned in the circle of his arms. "That's because I'm taking the bed," she emphasized. "*You* get the floor."

"Now let's think about this. I have a very big bed," he drawled, the cadence of his voice as smooth as silk, as slow as honey. "It's so big it'll be just as if you're on the other side of the room."

"You bet I'll be on the other side of the room," Sunny retorted, her eyes flashing and her mouth set in a kissable catch-me-if-you-can pout.

"We can be together, but not together," he whispered conspiratorially.

"Brett…"

From the corner of his eye, Brett saw his father edge into the doorway. Might as well make this good, he silently reasoned. "Yes, darling?" he said softly, leaning closer to Sunny's angelic features and brushing the hair back from her forehead before hooking one wispy tendril behind her ear.

Sunny's eyes widened in surprise. She imperceptibly glanced sideways to where his father stood, watching the tender, but orchestrated, scene.

Brett immediately drew her against him, body to body. Her attention swung back to him as heat magnified, fanning a deep-seated desire. Looping his arms around the small of her back, he pulled her as close as he could. Her breasts flattened to his broad chest, and she instinctively wriggled against him, curving her arms around his shoulders, his neck.

Her head tipped back and she gazed up at him, a glimmer of starlight in her confused gaze. Nuzzling her cheek, her nose, he bent down to brush his lips against her soft, full flesh. To kiss her as she was meant to be kissed, satisfy her as he longed to be sated. Her lips parted to allow him entrance, and he deepened the kiss.

Hearing a gurgle of pleasure in the back of her throat, he moved in delectable circles. Somewhere in the midst of the poignant, searing kiss, the charade ended and a misty, lose-yourself-to-reality came to be.

The embrace became mutual. The kiss became seductively intimate, provocatively intense. Sunny kissed him with her whole heart. He could feel it. And it scared the bloody hell out of him.

He'd had no idea feelings could run so deep. He'd had no idea that he could want her so much, so badly. He'd started this as a game, and it wasn't turning out that way at all. It was turning into the most impossible experience— of learning and longing and liking.

Liking someone more than you ever thought possible; liking the idea of spending time together…an indefinite amount of time, without restraint or constraint. Liking the way she smiled and laughed. Arguing points you didn't want to argue, just to hear the tinkly sound of her voice, the inflection that gave you goose bumps, the lilt that made you feel alive. On the inside, where it counted, and where it might be remembered for an eternity.

Brett heard his father clear his throat, but the noise sounded faraway. He was still tasting Sunny and tormenting himself when he realized vaguely that his father was announcing his presence. And he'd had to clear his throat not once, but twice!

Using every ounce of willpower, Brett reluctantly pulled away, his lips leaving hers. Yet he tasted her in his mouth, her scent lingered in his nostrils, his fingers knew her warmth, her curves.

In one impulsive moment, he had unwittingly crossed a line—and he wasn't sure there would ever be any going back.

Chapter Nine

"**I** may be a gentleman, but I am *not* sleeping on the floor," Brett declared. "And neither are you."

Sunny eyed the large, imposing bed, and a tremor of uncertainty scuttled up her spine. "Why is it," she asked, "that everything around you seems to be linked to royalty?"

Brett frowned. "What? What does that have to do with anything?"

"The bed. Is it a king? Or a queen?"

Brett's eyes dropped to the mattress. Then the corner of his mouth started to lift.

God, she hated it when he did that. It was so sexy. So riveting to watch the way he always broke into a smile, those innocent blue eyes twinkling.

"And isn't there a phrase for it?" she persisted. "Something about who you're making your bed with, or who you're crawling into bed with?"

"Me," he stated firmly, his smile disappearing. "You're crawling into bed with me." The statement was bald, decisive and unadorned. Then he tempered it. "For a king's ransom. Free room and board."

Sunny took a deep, steadying breath. If only he hadn't kissed her. She knew it had been for his father's benefit. But still...

"I agreed to help you out...but I never imagined this," she said.

"And me?" His gaze shamelessly trailed over the cherry-red nightgown, leaving smoldering heat everywhere his eyes had touched. "I never imagined *that*."

Inside, Sunny quivered, and her flesh prickled, becoming flash points of awareness, cognizance. She refused to surrender to those feelings. She swore she would overcome this unexpected thrust of desire, this need for intimacy. This was a crazy fling, nothing more. "I haven't anything else. I threw out my flannels," she grumbled. "After you made fun of them."

"I didn't make fun of them," he objected. "I merely thought something more provocative would be in order."

"*Provocative* is not a good word to use," she warned, inclining her head and unconsciously twisting the ring. "Not tonight."

They stood there, at an impasse. Neither one of them making a move, neither one inclined to pull back the covers and crawl between the sheets. It had been one thing to know she'd slept in beds he owned, on pillows that he had purchased. But to sleep in *his* bed, to listen to his even breathing, to imagine what he would look like when he awoke? It was too much. All of it.

She'd never get a wink of sleep. She'd worry their toes were going to bump in the night. Or that his leg might brush hers. Or that she'd turn to reach for the extra pillow she always slept with—and pull him close to her instead!

God, this was awful. It was awful and wonderful. It was excruciating torment; it was unbearable intimacy.

It was Brett Hamilton, shirtless. Wearing the bottoms of black silk pajamas. The elastic waist sagged below his navel. It rode his hips and accentuated an all-male, raw virility.

"Is that uncomfortable?" Brett asked suddenly. "Because if it is, you can always take it off."

"What!"

"The ring," he said quickly. "You're always turning that ring every time you get nervous."

She jerked her hand down and briefly stared at it, as if it was a wake-up call. "I'm not nervous."

"Of course you are."

"And why would you think that?" she challenged, lifting her chin and defiantly meeting his unwavering blue gaze.

"Because—" he lifted a shoulder, the muscles working beneath his skin in a mysterious, inviting fashion "—I am, too."

Hearing his confession weakened Sunny's defenses one more notch. "Well, we're just going to *sleep* together. You've got your clothes on—" her gaze inadvertently drifted to the silk that barely covered his male anatomy "—I've got mine on. It's not like—"

"Sunny."

"What?"

"Don't say another word. Please." He reached for the comforter, bunching it in his fist before he dragged it down to expose erotic black cotton sheets. "You're just making it worse. We're talking about sex, even though we're not talking about sex."

"I most certainly was not."

"But we're both thinking about it. Or at least we're conscious of it. There's always this...this thing between men and women."

"But not between us."

"Of course not," he insisted.

Sunny glanced at his bed, imagining him in it. She reached for her side of the comforter, the blankets, and slowly drew them down, new conviction rising in her. She could do this. She could keep him, and her errant fantasy, at arm's length.

"We'll think about the sightseeing tour we plan to take my parents on tomorrow," he suggested, putting a knee on the bed and crawling in. "We'll think about where we're going to eat and how we're going to entertain them. We won't think about how uncomfortable this situation is." He rolled on his back and pulled the covers up across his chest before stacking his hands behind his head. He looked up at her expectantly.

Sunny followed suit. Without saying a word, she climbed into bed beside Brett Hamilton, the office heartthrob. She lay on her back, stiffly, and stared at the ceiling. His ceiling. Where thousands of stars seemed to sparkle, and taunt and tease.

Taking a deep breath, she became inordinately conscious of her breasts. Her breasts, of all things! And how they put two distinctive mounds beneath the comforter next to him. How her breasts rose and fell with every breath she took. She wondered if he noticed. She wondered if he knew they ached beneath her self-conscious scrutiny, that they tingled for a loving touch.

Neither she nor Brett spoke. Finally, after what seemed aeons, he reached over and turned out the bedside light.

The darkness seemed to magnify the raspy sounds of Brett settling in for the night. The way he straightened the covers, the way he moved his arm, dropping it stiffly between them like the bundling board of the New England colonials.

Sunny crossed her arms over her middle and pinned the blankets down, nervously raking a fingernail along the satin piping on the comforter.

"I can't sleep," Brett said finally.

"Me, either."

"Do you suppose," he said carefully, "that if I put my arm out like this—" Sunny felt his arm lift and raise, to settle at the back of her pillow "—that you could just put your head on it, and we could both get over this ridiculous fear of accidentally touching each other in the middle of the night?''

The invitation, genuinely given, didn't really require an answer. Sunny considered, then eased nearer to him and allowed her nape to settle into the crook of his arm. Her shoulder fit beneath the hollow of his as they both turned to accommodate the other.

He felt so warm. He smelled even better, like soap and aftershave and starchy dress shirts. His chest was like a big, comfortable pillow that she wanted to snuggle up next to.

The silence, which moments before had been so awkward, became comfortable, companionable.

''Sunny?''

''Yes?''

''You're being a really good sport. About everything. This ruse, about getting out of one relationship, seems to have inadvertently found me another. I feel closer to you than I ever could have to Lady Harriet. I'm convinced I could spend a lifetime with that woman and not know her as well as I've gotten to know you in one week. You've made me realize I've made the right choice and I'm doing the right thing. I don't suppose I'll ever be able to repay you, not for what it's worth, but I do want to thank you.''

Sunny's heart thrummed. It was a small thing, this thank-you. But it would be something to carry away with her. She was going to need some kind of comfort when this was all over, for he aroused too much within her, and she didn't know, really, how she would ever return to her single, solitary life.

Breakfast had been one uncomfortable nightmare. Sunny swore that Lady Hamilton kept looking at her as if to say ''How dare you live with my son.''

To make up for it, Sunny knocked herself out making Belgian waffles and cappuccino while Brett showed them around the apartment. At the table, Lady Miriam took a polite sip of the cappuccino, then remarked that Sunny shouldn't have gone to so much trouble; she would have been satisfied with a good pot of tea.

Lord Arthur exclaimed over the waffles, then promptly scraped all of the strawberry sauce off. Too much for his indigestion, he explained.

Brett had immediately launched into a diatribe about Sunny's mother's zucchini pancakes, and his parents had listened with faint interest. Finally, his mother commented, "Zucchini? That is a rather common vegetable, isn't it?"

"Yes, very ordinary," Sunny remarked, offering Brett an adoring smile. "But my mom makes it special." It occurred to Sunny at that moment that his parents had not yet asked about hers; they didn't seem to want to know anything about her or her background.

Brett patted the back of her hand. "Breakfast was wonderful. As usual, darling," he praised. "Sunny loves to dote on me," he confided. "She spoils me terribly."

Both his parents looked at Brett and smiled indulgently, as if they had produced a child who didn't know what he really wanted or what was good for him.

"I thought we'd walk the Freedom Trail today," he suggested. "It's a nice day and we can walk and talk, and all get to know each other. Besides, it's a great way to see Boston," he enthused.

Lady Miriam looked at her plate and silently chased a bite of waffle around it.

"If you'd like, my boy, I can hire a driver," Lord Arthur magnanimously offered.

"Not necessary. We'll take a cab to the trail, then walk it. There's quite a bit to see, actually. It will be invigorating."

"Adventuresome." Sunny chimed in, picking up on Brett's exuberance. "You'll get the flavor of old Boston."

"But, children," Lady Miriam protested, "we really didn't come to see Boston, we came to see…about our son," she said pointedly.

"You'll see me, Mother! Me, and the old city of Boston. Come along. We'll have a grand time."

"Yes, well…you always did like to have a rollicking good time, didn't you?" She smiled affectionately at him and reached for the strawberry syrup Sunny offered for her waffle. Instead of taking it, she fixed her gaze on the diamond ring glittering on Sunny's finger. "Oh. I quite forgot about *that*. It was so late last night and we were so…surprised at Brett's sudden engagement that I didn't really see it well."

Sunny put the syrup down and extended her hand for his mother's inspection.

"It wasn't sudden, Mother. Sunny has been at Wintersoft for at least two years, but I only really got to know her when I moved here six months ago, to Boston."

"I just love the ring," Sunny said, realizing it wasn't a lie. "Although we picked it out together, Brett did surprise me with it. I wasn't expecting it. Not at all."

"Neither were we, my dear," Lord Arthur stated. "Neither were we."

"It's rather…dainty, isn't it?" his mother carefully observed, tilting the stone beneath the light.

"We call it our 'starter' ring," Brett joked. "Like some young couples have their starter homes."

"Yes, well, and it might be the only one you'll ever be able to afford," his father predicted dimly.

Sunny pulled her hand back slowly, knowing full well that Brett's inheritance hung in the balance. It was her job to sway them, to convince them he should marry a woman of his dreams, even if it ultimately wasn't her.

They started the tour at Boston Common, a forty-four acre park near Tremont Street. They passed the State House, Park Street Church and the Granary Burying Ground. Lord and Lady Hamilton caught on quite quickly that the thrust of the tour highlighted the colonials fight for freedom from the British. As a result they were not particularly amused, or enamored.

They stopped in the Quincy Market for lunch, but Lady Miriam picked at her food and seemed fixated by the token Sunny wore on her left hand, fourth finger.

Paul Revere's home, just around the corner from the Haymarket, was one more stopping point in their self-guided tour. Brett winked mischievously and mimicked Revere's famous cry, "The British are coming! The British are coming!"

Both of his parents smiled faintly, but it was his mother who said, "I've had about enough lessons in American history, Brett dear. That, and my feet hurt from doing so. Can we save the rest for another visit?"

Brett shrugged his shoulders and immediately hailed a cab. Once inside, he directed the cabbie to the infamous Boston Harbor. "I thought you'd like to see where the Boston Tea Party took place," he said. "The colonials painted themselves up like Indians, swam into the harbor and dumped tons of tea into the water."

His father stared into the murky depths. "Dreadful waste of good tea, wasn't it?" he remarked drolly. "And a very impulsive act. Of course, some impulsive things can be undone." He offered Brett a significant look, and even Sunny guessed at the message.

Yet Brett was undaunted and reached for Sunny's hand, capturing it within his. "Some things are meant to be, Father. Just as some things are meant to be done, and not undone." He let a fraction of a second slip away, and then, as if his prophecy had never been uttered, added, "You'll love the restaurant we've chosen for dinner tonight. We'll have just enough time to change and rest up at the apartment. It will be an unforgettable evening for the four of us. I promise you."

Chapter Ten

It was obvious to Brett that his parents had no intention of liking Sunny. They either ignored her or listened politely and then dismissed her. It was disheartening to see the way Sunny tried so hard to win their approval. He felt sorry for her. But Sunny, true to her name, just kept smiling.

She had knocked herself out getting ready for dinner. It had been a challenge, actually, juggling private moments in the bedroom they now shared so that they could dress separately without letting on to his parents.

He had been the last to dress, and doing so had put him in one of those naughty and nice moments, full of intoxicating temptation and curious awareness. Sunny had apparently stepped out of her low-heeled walking shoes in his closet, and the shoes stood there, paired, on the claret-colored carpet. They were sensible shoes, yes, but there was something about them…

He tied his tie and realized he didn't know what it was that nagged him about her shoes. His gaze kept drifting over to them. The shiny black piping on the toe. Or the soft, smooth leather. Fashioned like a slipper, they added an interestingly feminine accent to the dark, bold colors he'd chosen for his bedroom. They looked, oddly, as if they belonged. He snapped the loose end of his tie harder than necessary and tried not to think of it.

In her haste, she'd strewn her clothes across his bed. The pant legs were in a twist, and the sleeve of her blouse had slithered down his side of the bed.

Huh. *His* side. Last night there had been a his and a hers side—and it never occurred to him to resent sharing any of it.

The fuzzy puddle of yarn on his pillow was her sweater, and he shrewdly guessed that later tonight, when he tried to sleep, he'd inhale her scent. He should have snatched it off his pillow, folded it and put it on the dresser. But he'd left it there, considering instead that he'd have dreams, the sweetest of dreams.

He yanked on his suit coat and strode out to the living room, where his parents and Sunny waited. Her back was to him, and she'd swiveled on her heel when she heard him enter the room.

She'd chosen to wear the cranberry-colored suit for their first dinner out—and he couldn't take his eyes off of her. The outfit was in classic good taste, but the pumps put a curvaceous suggestion on the arch of her foot and the calf of her leg.

Something inside him went primal, and a little voice in the back of his head screamed, "sexy, sexy, sexy!"

She'd put her tawny-streaked hair up, in some knotty little thing at the back of her head, but loose tendrils kept falling away, at her temple, her nape. They framed her face and made his fingers itch, he wanted so badly to brush them back, to wind one tender little curl around his pinky. The pearls added the finishing touch to the prim-and-proper image she was trying to project, but he noted that she fingered them occasionally, as if for reassurance.

"You look lovely tonight," he murmured softly. "Darling," he added in an afterthought, as he buzzed her cheek.

She smelled like baby powder and some seductive scent that had a hint of musk, a hint of vanilla. Giving in to the impulse, he snagged one of the tendrils in front of her ear and tweaked it. "Putting your hair up is particularly sexy, luv," he whispered, a notch louder than he needed to. "Are you trying to drive me insane?"

His parents heard. He knew they did. For his mother sniffed and his father rattled the ice cubes in his glass.

But it was Sunny's response that was so mesmerizing. She offered him the most demure look. A smile curved gently upward, and her eyes widened, the blue irises flaring with color. He watched with bemused pleasure as her lashes fluttered, nearly touching her eyebrows.

The compliment had surprised her, but the heavy innuendo had aroused a flame inside of her. He could see it— the soft glow highlighting her features, the radiating heat that seemed nearly palpable.

"Are we ready, then?" his father asked, a shred of petulance in his voice.

"We really don't have time to dilly-dally," his mother chided. "The taxi should be here any moment."

Brett reluctantly dragged his gaze away. For a moment it shocked him to realize he wasn't pretending, either. He had the strangest urge to sit and admire Sunny, to look into the warm depths of her eyes and steal a fortifying glimpse of her soul.

Ignoring his parents, he reverently lifted the dark blue dress coat that Sunny had laid over the back of a chair, and helped her slip it on. He lingered attentively at her collar, smoothing the seams at her shoulders and brushing away an imaginary speck of lint.

"Brett, come along," his mother insisted. "I'm sure Sunny can manage."

He swiveled. "But I absolutely adore waiting on her." Snagging her hand, he possessively tucked it in his and steered her to the door.

His parents exchanged a can-you-believe-this? look and

walked ahead of them, out the door. The cab waited at
the curb.

"I'm doing my best, Brett, really. But I'm afraid your
parents don't like me at all," Sunny whispered, while he
locked the door.

"Hush," he said. "By the end of the evening, I promise
that they're going to be mad about you."

Sunny cast him a doubtful look, but stoically put her
game face back on the minute they were inside the cab. On
the way to The Club, a posh restaurant in Cambridge,
Sunny said all the right things. She told his mother that she
had a fervent desire to see where Brett had grown up. She
asked about Phillip's little girls, and successfully remembered all their names and ages. She engaged his father in
a discussion about his hunting dogs.

But his parents refused to budge. They were civil, tight-
lipped and cool.

Poor Sunny, Brett thought dismally. She was knocking
herself out against something that was akin to the white
cliffs of Dover. Impenetrable, impossible and stone-faced.

Once inside the restaurant, they were immediately seated,
and Brett went overboard, lavishly ordering an expensive
bottle of wine and an extravagant tray of appetizers. His
mother picked at the tray, and his father tested the bouquet
of the wine, then shrugged. Sunny unabashedly dived into
the crab-stuffed lobster croquettes.

Some minutes passed in utter and desolate silence.

Sunny fidgeted, probably because his parents were such
a hard sell and she was running out of things to say. "Oh,
my, those are so rich," she finally exclaimed, fanning herself delicately above the breast. "I really need to excuse
myself for a visit to the powder room."

His father looked slightly askance, but Brett's gaze
trailed after Sunny, wondering if she was giving up the
ship. He wouldn't blame her if she did; his parents had
been completely uncooperative to her overtures.

"Brett, we need to talk," his father said firmly. "Now. While we're alone."

"Breton, this entire charade is preposterous," his mother added. Brett started and glanced at his mother warily, wondering if she had seen through the ruse. "You simply need to rethink this engagement. It's not too late to call it off."

"What?" Brett looked from his mother to his father and back again.

"Brett, if you continue with this, I shall have no other choice but to cut you off from your inheritance. Your grandfather's estate is pending, and the monies can be withdrawn at my discretion."

"Father, I don't care about the money. It could give me a comfortable life, but I've come to realize I can be happy without an inheritance. I'd far rather marry a woman of my own choosing."

"Breton, listen to yourself!" his mother chided. "There's nothing wrong with this girl, but you are in a position to have it all. A lovely wife, a handsome inheritance, a title. Lady Harriet would take you back in a minute."

"Mother!"

"It's true," she said evenly, raising both eyebrows for emphasis.

"And an alliance between our families would be nothing to scoff at, Breton. It would be a prudent financial move," his father reminded him.

"And the social registers would cough up double time," his mother said airily.

"Combined, our assets would be in the high millions."

"I don't want to be on any social register," Brett argued. "And I don't love Lady Harriet. I can't imagine being married to her, not for a million-plus dollars." He stared them both down. "I *want* Sunny," he said defiantly.

"Don't be foolish, son. Think what you're giving up!" His mother lifted both hands, her fingers spread, her jewels glittering. "You'll regret this," she warned.

"No, I won't. Because…because…" Logic had vanished. Brett was tired of fighting, weary of the same old worn-out arguments. His parents couldn't see his side, and he couldn't see theirs. He looked away, his gaze fastening on a plump, very pregnant female who was negotiating her way, belly first, among the tables. "Because," he said finally, "there may be a baby. And I could never leave Sunny at a time like this."

A sharp intake of air rasped through his mother's lips. His father sat immobile, his drink suspended in midair. "I do say, Breton…"

"She'll be a good mother, don't you think?" Brett asked hopefully, casting longing eyes to the closed door of the powder room. "She's so tenderhearted. So lovable and caring."

"Brett, you aren't serious? A baby…?"

"Phillip's girls—Elizabeth, GeorgeAnn, Margaret and the new baby—they'll have a cousin."

His father harrumphed, but Brett could see his stoic reserve was crumbling. "This isn't the way we do things, you know," Lord Arthur said sternly.

"I know, I know. But sometimes things happen. And maybe they happen for the best. And you love them, anyway. Or more than you ever thought possible."

"Ah, Brett…I wish you'd told us…." His mother looked torn.

"I wanted you to get to know Sunny first. She is a wonderful girl, Mother."

"I can see you think that, yes. But—"

"If you'd just give her a chance."

His mother heaved an aggrieved sigh. The same one she'd issued before she'd fired each of his nannies.

"We have always wanted the best for you, my boy."

"Arthur," his mother intervened, "perhaps we have been too hard on Sunny. If Brett is willing to give up all for her, then…well…" She left the rest unsaid.

His father tossed back the remainder of his wine. "We'll

need some time to think on this, I'm afraid. A baby complicates things. It changes things.''

Brett looked over to see Sunny heading toward the table. ''Here she is. Don't let on. Please. We haven't told anyone yet, and—''

''We certainly don't intend to tell anyone, either,'' his father said dryly, beckoning for the waiter to bring them more wine.

''Oh, my, it's stuffy in here, don't you think?'' Sunny asked, sliding into her chair and simultaneously fanning herself. ''It helped to move around. I can't imagine what's the matter with me.''

Brett watched his mother's eyes roam over Sunny's midsection as she leaned back in the chair. His father tried not to look, but sent surreptitious glances over her plate. ''That food's pretty rich,'' he said. ''And maybe you shouldn't be drinking.''

''Oh, I don't drink at all, really,'' Sunny protested. ''Only on special occasions. And tonight is a special occasion, to have you here with Brett and myself.''

''He means…'' Lady Miriam paused. ''That it might not be good for you.''

Sunny looked surprised. ''Oh? I thought a glass of wine was supposed to be good for the heart.''

His mother vehemently shook her head. ''Not under the circumstances. If you…aren't feeling well.''

''Well, I've never felt better,'' Sunny announced with a brilliant smile. She picked up her wine flute, extending it in a mock toast. ''Good food, good company, good—''

Lord Hamilton snagged the glass right out of her fingers. ''That will be enough, my dear,'' he said. ''We don't want you to overdo.''

Sunny, looking positively baffled, allowed her empty right hand to drop limply on the table. It was obvious she didn't know whether she was being chastised or cared for.

''You'll only be that much warmer with wine,'' Brett explained soothingly, patting the back of her knuckles.

"Oh. Well…"

"Tell me, Sunny," his mother said, readjusting the linen napkin on her lap. "Do you have siblings? Nieces? Nephews?"

"No. I was an only child," she admitted, a note of longing in her voice. "I used to beg Doug and Syl for a baby."

"Doug and Syl?"

"Oh." Sunny spread her hands in embarrassment. "My parents. Of course, I call them Mom and Dad, too, but there are times I just think of them as Doug and Sylvia. I'm not trying to be rude or anything, because we have this adult relationship and—"

His mother put up her hand like a mock stop sign. "I understand, I understand. No need for a lengthy explanation. I merely wondered if you had spent any time around, say, young children?"

"No. Not at all. I wanted brothers and sisters terribly. But my parents believed in that one-point-eight children in a family thing. And since eight-tenths isn't a whole, they settled for me," she tried to joke. Brett winced when his parents didn't get it. Sunny, unfazed, added, "My parents used to call me the house mom to the all the stray dogs and cats I could bring home, though. I've bottle-fed litters of kittens and stayed up with sick dogs, and—"

A pained expression crossed his mother's face. "Yes, well, Sunny…caring for animals is not quite the same as caring for a *baby*."

"Oh, I know. But I figure I'm working my way up to it. I hope by then I know the difference between litter training a kitty and potty training an infant."

Brett choked. He slapped a napkin over his mouth and reached for the bottle of wine at the same time. He needed to fortify himself, for Sunny was positively glowing when she made the unwitting remark.

"From flea powder to baby powder," Sunny continued, undaunted and uninformed.

His parents stared at her.

Brett slung an arm around her shoulders. "Sunny is such a nurturing person. She just loves to care for all those helpless creatures."

His mother dabbed at her mouth with her napkin. "Brett's brother, Phillip, is an excellent father," she said proudly. "I'm certain Brett will be, too."

"Even so. It's a huge commitment to parent a child," his father said humorlessly as he drilled Sunny with an unwavering gaze.

"Of course, they're worth every minute. But you have to have values, standards." The first smile Lady Miriam had chosen to bestow on Sunny was thin, brittle. "Children need routine. They need to know limits, and what is expected of them. Babies are wonderful, but they do turn into children."

Sunny fell silent, confusion riddling her brow.

"Mother—"

"I'm just saying—" his mother shrugged "—that child-rearing techniques can be so different, due to culture and station."

"That's true," Sunny said. "But my parents were pretty unorthodox—or innovative, depending on which way you choose to look at it—and I think I turned out okay."

"You turned out more than okay, darling," Brett gushed quickly, intent on stemming the thrust of the conversation. "Mother, Father? Isn't she just the most smashing woman? I could have looked a lifetime and not found someone like Sunny."

"That's true, son," his father agreed philosophically, as he nodded and poured more wine into his flute. "Instead you've set your own course, apparently into uncharted territories."

His mother sniffed and looked suspiciously misty-eyed. "It's just…you're such children yourselves. And you've known each other for such a short time. It's hard to imagine—"

"That people could fall so head over heels in love like

Sunny and I did?'' Brett interrupted, half-afraid his mother would use the word *baby* aloud.

"It's not the falling in love, Breton,'' his mother replied. "It's apparently what it now entails.''

Chapter Eleven

Sunny stood with her back to Brett and brushed her hair while she looked out his bedroom window. The view, a tranquil panorama of the playground, only made her more agitated. She considered the swings and slide and wondered what his parents were thinking—that they would accept her if she offered herself up as a baby machine?

"What in the world was going on tonight, Brett?" she asked suddenly, turning to face him. To her horror, he was wearing only a skinny little pair of briefs. "Oh! Oh, I..."

"You needn't be embarrassed. I often wear a whole lot less when I'm swimming."

Sunny fought to control the damp heat suffusing her body. "Of course. Remind me to start swimming when we break up, just so I can get an occasional glimpse of you."

An amused grin stole onto Brett's face. "You are wicked," he whispered. "Remind me to torment you Mondays, Wednesdays and Fridays, in the lap pool."

The look Brett sent her was hot, sexy and very inviting. *The look.* Sunny needed to remind herself to avoid it, to avoid harboring memories of it in her heart. Nothing was going to happen, nothing ever would happen, nothing was intended to happen.

"About tonight," she began again, determined to stay on track. "They were very stuck on babies, weren't they? I got the impression your parents would accept almost anything if it meant you provided them with an heir."

"That's because…" Brett took a deep breath. "I led them to believe there could be a baby on the way. You know. You. Me. And a baby."

"A what?"

"Baby." The rocking gesture he made with his arms seemed incongruous against his bare chest, above the skimpy briefs.

"You told them I was pregnant?"

His arms dropped. "Well, not in so many words."

"I don't care how many words it took!"

"I hinted."

Sunny dropped the brush on the nightstand and sank, knees first, onto the bed. "They think I'm going to have a baby. That's why they were so nice to me." She twisted to look up at him, unaware how the move pulled her gown revealingly across her breast, waist and hip. "You have to tell them the truth. I won't be able to look them in the eye in the morning. They'll think we're—we're…" She fluttered a hand over the expanse of bedding between them.

He sat on the mattress opposite her. "Well, that is what couples usually do when they're living together, my dear."

"Well, we're not. I'm doing you a favor, not sleeping with you."

"You did last night."

"Last night was different."

A slow, thoughtful smile creased his face. "It was, wasn't it?"

"Brett. I'm being serious."

"I am, too." He slid the covers down and crawled beneath, indicating she should do the same. "Come on. Let's talk about it. Like we did last night. I once heard all couples talk about everything in bed. Shall we try it?''

Sunny wanted to be exasperated with him, but she couldn't. It was all she could do not to smile. He was a tease. He teased constantly.

"You can have my shoulder again and complain about being preggers. And I could rub your tummy and—''

"You will not!''

He laughed. "But I want to. I watched you sitting across the table from me tonight and it hit me how you would look pregnant, with a baby. Have you ever thought of that?''

"Brett, this is outrageous, to talk like this.''

"So?'' His look was devilish, and he patted the pillow next to him. "It's my bedroom and I can talk about whatever I want here. And if you're sharing my bed, I can talk about it with you. A confidence. Between us.''

Sunny reluctantly stretched out beside him and drew the covers up to her middle. Her head rested uncomfortably against the pillow. She missed his arm, but she'd never admit it.

The moment she thought it, he extended his arm, silently inviting her to move against him, as she'd done the night before. "Tell me. What do you think about babies?'' he said softly.

"I think,'' she said, nestling her head against his shoulder, "they have their time and place. And I want a houseful. With the right man, of course.''

"A houseful.''

"Mmm.'' Her eyes drifted closed and she found a sense of peace, even as she wondered vaguely how they were going to get out of this mess with his parents. "Did you,'' she ventured, "ever think of having children with Lady Harriet?''

"What?'' He stiffened slightly.

"Well, your parents mention her all the time. She must

have been the perfect person. Probably the perfect mother. You dated her.''

He chuckled. ''You sound positively jealous.''

''Don't be ridiculous.'' A second passed. ''I was just wondering. I feel like I can't possibly measure up. Besides, if I am supposedly carrying your baby, I feel I have the right to know what went on between you and Lady Harriet. You owe me that much.''

He laughed, and it was some moments before his chuckles subsided. ''Sunny?'' He turned to face her, lifting up on one elbow. The movement emphasized the expanse of his chest, his powerful shoulders, thick neck and muscular arms. His fingertips settled on her abdomen, stroking a path down the middle. ''Even if you wind up a little plump in your pregnancy, you more than measure up,'' he said huskily. ''You are far more sexy and far more appealing.'' Two hearts thudded in the night. ''Forget Lady Harriet,'' he whispered, ''for nothing happened between her and me. Nothing of consequence. And I'm very glad it didn't. Otherwise there might not be you.''

In the end Sunny had agreed to play more than his fiancée; she had agreed to play his pregnant live-in lover. To heighten the illusion, Brett became more attentive. He offered her his chair. He asked if she was tired, if she needed a nap. He made quite a to-do over seeing that there was a serving of milk beside her plate at every meal, then he'd pat her hand and remind her she needed her calcium.

His parents bought into it, hook, line and sinker.

It had been four days, and not only was Sunny beginning to feel like the ultimate fraud, she was beginning to eye maternity dresses and white-painted nursery furniture. They began nudging each other every time a rosy-cheeked cherub crossed their path. The entire scenario had gone beyond ludicrous. But it was deliciously fun to imagine each other as parent material—even as Sunny privately told Brett they needed to put a stop to it.

Lord Arthur and Lady Miriam had thawed. A little. They were civil to Sunny, even though an aura of disapproval hung about them, as heavy as a cloak.

"You haven't told us much about your parents," Lady Miriam said one night at dinner. "What do they do?"

Sunny panicked. Her parents had done a lot of everything and not much of anything. "They, um—" her mind fought for a logical, acceptable answer "—they are into home care products. Like soap. And candles. They have their own company."

A flicker of interest scudded through Lord Arthur's eyes. "Really? They aren't with the R&D Group, are they?"

R&D had made the Forbes list last year as the fastest growing, most profitable enterprise in North America. Sunny guessed there wasn't a kitchen in America that didn't have some kind of product they manufactured. She waved away the implication. "Oh, no. No, not quite that large."

"Sunny's parents have developed all-natural products," Brett interjected helpfully.

"In today's competitive markets, it helps to have a niche."

"This is just a little niche," Sunny clarified, holding her thumb and forefinger a fraction of an inch apart.

"I'd like to meet your father, Sunny," Lord Arthur announced.

She caught her breath. It was either that or fall off the chair.

"And I'd love to meet your mother," Lady Miriam stated. "It seems only appropriate."

"Oh…" Sunny practically strangled. She took a long draft of the thing closest to her elbow, milk, and tried again. "Oh, they're on the road a lot. Traveling, you know."

Lady Miriam looked at her blankly. "I thought you said they were in Boston now."

"Oh." Her brain tripped backward, recalling what she'd

said, and momentarily short-circuited. "They are. They're between trips right now."

"Then, tomorrow night?"

"Meetings," Sunny said quickly. Tomorrow night *was* Doug's meditation class. That would make a plausible excuse. "He has these things on…broadening your horizons, making the most of your inner energy."

"Interesting. The man's a self-starter, then."

Sunny moved her glass of milk. It was either that or throw it. "You could say that. I think they're…successful…because they don't do things the conventional way."

"Successful?" Lady Miriam perked up. "That is a compliment. We absolutely must meet them. I insist. Since we'll be in Boston a few more days we surely must get together."

"Oh, well, they don't do the fancy things. They don't belong to a country club or—"

"Sunny's parents are wonderful people," Brett chimed in. "Very down to earth. And so interesting."

"That settles it," Lord Arthur declared. "I'm sure they are wondering about us, wondering if our family is good enough for their daughter."

"Oh," Sunny began to protest, "I don't think that's an issue—"

"There's a wonderful family restaurant over near the Cape. A little out-of-the-way place I discovered," Brett suggested smoothly. "Very casual. We could do something informal. Dress down and relax."

"A marvelous idea," Lady Miriam gushed. "Do call them, Sunny, right now."

They were seated at a round table, but Sunny felt cornered. She looked around, and realized she had no choice but to agree.

"You're sure this place isn't going to be too expensive?" Sunny's mother asked. "Things are a little tight for us right now. And I'd hate to pay $12.95 for a salad."

Sunny clutched the phone, wondering if all her angst ould subside if her parents backed out. But she really anted them to go. It might be good for them to see how e other half of the world lived. She was convinced Brett's rents and hers were at the opposite ends of the spectrum d diametrically opposed to each other. Of course, maybe they spent an evening together they'd find some middle ound.

"I've never been there, but Brett says it's something spe- al. Very elegant and upscale. Don't worry about how uch it costs. It's his treat. He wants his parents to enjoy emselves and he's so appreciative of me helping them d their way around Boston that he wants to include you." nny paused. "You are dressing up, aren't you?"

"Basic black. You know. Dress it up, dress it down."

Sunny cringed, her eyes shuttering closed, even as she ped for the best. Still, she doubted that the outfit would svèlte, or rhinestone studded.

"Don't be late," she warned. "Brett's hired a car for six clock."

"We won't be late, Sunny. My goodness, you don't have look after us."

"I know. I just—" Sunny broke off, unsure she could l her mother what she was really thinking. "I just want ings to go well. It means a lot to me."

"Honey, we love you. We want you to be happy. Why, it meant spending our nest egg over dinner tonight, we'd it."

"I know you would," Sunny said miserably. Dammit. hy did she always have to feel so torn where her parents ere concerned? "But I have to tell you something," she id, staring at the diamond ring on her finger. "About rett's parents, and this get-together and…"

"Yes?"

Sunny dropped her hand. She'd worry about the ring

later. She'd wear gloves or keep her hand under the tab
in her lap, in her pocket. Whatever. But she simply couldr
bring herself to tell them she was wearing a diamond Br
had put on her finger. Taking a deep, rejuvenating breat
she plunged forward with the explanation. "They've cor
all the way from England, and they're very British. *Ve*
British," she emphasized. "So could you warn Doug th
Brett may introduce them as—" she cleared her thro
"—Lord Arthur and Lady Miriam?"

Charged silence filled her revelation. Then her moth
asked carefully, "Do you suppose that Brett could ju
mumble his way through that part? I wouldn't want Dou
to say something about the royal caste system of subjug
tion, serfdom and servitude."

"I wouldn't want him to say it, either, Mom. Particular
because I'm so happy to have a friend like Brett, who
such a nice guy. A regular guy, in spite of his title."

"He has one, too?"

"That's the way it usually works, Mom. It's hand
down from one generation to the next."

"Well, don't worry, dear. Some things can be ove
come."

Her mother's reply wasn't particularly comforting, b
Sunny was determined to get through the evening with tl
four of them. She swore she would make this work, r
matter if it killed her.

She'd done all the right things to set it up. She'd me
tioned little details about her parents to Lord Arthur ar
Lady Miriam. Like how they actually lived in the san
apartment complex, because they didn't like to be tie
down keeping up a larger place. She'd casually mentione
that because of their business they were particularly co
cerned about environmental issues.

Her parents, to her relief, were right on time. Althoug
Doug visibly blanched when he was introduced to Lo
Arthur and Lady Miriam, he nodded firmly, clamping h
lips over any untoward commentary about social hierarch

Her mother shook hands all around while Doug kissed Sunny on the cheek.

"What do you think, Sunshine?" he asked, modeling a long-sleeved, cocoa-colored dress shirt. "New threads."

"Nice. Very nice," Sunny approved. "But you've got—" she reached to his breast pocket, to pull at a loose thread "a—"

His father looked down. "Oops. Missed one." He plucked at the thread. "Charlie gave it to me. From the Donut Kitchen. They were getting new uniforms. All we had to do was take off this little patch—" he swiped at the spot where the Donut Kitchen logo had once been firmly stitched "—and voilà! A pretty distinctive shirt, wouldn't you say?"

"I…"

Doug extended his arm to Lady Miriam. "Feel this fabric," he insisted. "Stain repellant. Wears like iron." Lady Miriam's eyes slowly traveled all the way down her nose, to settle on the polyester-cotton blend covering her father's forearm. "Good stuff. Practical and no-nonsense. Can't wait to see what our new soap does with this."

A flicker of awareness brightened her gaze. "Oh. I see," she said in apparent relief, awkwardly patting the cuff of his shirt. "An experiment. With your new product."

Lord Arthur laughed heartily. When confusion rolled through Doug's eyes, Sunny said quickly, "I told them you and Mom were into soap and candles."

"That we are," Sylvia said proudly. "We've got quite an assembly line going."

"Marketing," Lord Arthur said, "that's the key these days."

"Yes, we're just popping up all over," Sylvia said. She produced a pair of raffia bound tapers. "I brought you a little something, Miriam," she said smoothly. "I thought maybe you could find a place for them in the castle."

"Castle?"

"Castle, estate." Brett broke in, shrugging. "Americans seem to use the terms interchangeably."

"Oh. Well, thank you. They smell so—" Lady Miriam frowned, then sniffed again "—nice."

"Honey and almond." Sylvia winked. "I promise you that will take the edge off any old drafty rooms."

"We can wait by the doors at the front of the building," Brett suggested. "The car should be here any minute."

The entourage strolled downstairs, making small talk, with Brett and Sunny intervening on any topic that could be potentially dangerous. Then they waited and waited. And waited.

Finally Brett called the company on his cellphone. "I'd ordered a limo...but they said they're having mechanical troubles. Should be here any minute."

They waited another five minutes. Lady Miriam complained that her feet were beginning to hurt. Sylvia drew the fringed black shawl a little more closely around her long, free-flowing peasant dress. It was gauzy cotton, and the temperature was dropping.

"If you're cold, Mom, we could wait in the apartment."

"Oh, don't worry about me, honey. I just have to be one with the elements. It's a state of mind, really."

Lady Miriam pinched the front of her fur coat together and glanced at Sylvia, obviously unconvinced.

Brett's cellphone rang and he answered it. "Bad news," he said a moment later, flipping it closed. "They've broke down again and haven't another limo available. Maybe I could call a cab, and we could take a cab and my car and—"

"Forget that," Doug said expansively. "We'll take my wheels. We'll all fit."

Before Sunny could throw herself in front of him, Doug bolted out the door, keys in hand. Sunny looked up at Brett, sheer horror glazing her eyes.

"Not a problem," Sylvia assured them. "It's not new, but it's got a good heater and there's more than enough room. And this way we won't have to wait. Otherwise we might lose our reservations.''

"Considering how long we've waited, I'd ride in about anything," Lady Miriam declared.

Sunny couldn't bring herself to tell her she was about to get her wish.

When her father came wheeling around the corner in their old pea-green VW bus, Brett's lips began to twitch.

The bus, a four-wheel memorial to the Grateful Dead, was adorned with peace symbols, rainbows and flowers. Faded curtains swung in all the windows, and rust speckled the sides.

"What is that?" Lady Miriam asked, her eyebrows raised and her eyes fixed on the silver hood ornament. "Not a BMW?''

A low chuckle rumbled through Brett's chest. "A VW," he said. "This time around consider it a vintage car."

A relieved smile broke through on Lord Arthur's face. "Vintage. Oh, well. That's different. It's a rather engaging vehicle, isn't it?''

Sunny whapped her hand against her forehead, unable to believe Brett's parents would buy into the scenario. The VW bus was little more than a scrap heap that for years had been held together with baling wire and duct tape.

"Sunny?" her mother said curiously. "What's that on your hand?''

Sunny's fingers, splayed, slowly inched down her face. The brilliance of the diamond was reflected in her mother's surprised eyes.

"Douglas! Look!" she called, drawing him out of the driver's seat. "Sunny's engaged!''

Chapter Twelve

"Let me propose a toast," Doug said, raising the arm of his Donut Kitchen dress shirt, a flute of champagne in hand. "To my little girl, and the man she's chosen to call her own. She's finally met the man of her dreams—and she always said when she met him she'd marry him! May they always be happy together, and may they always enjoy the *Kama Sutra* pleasures of the marriage bed."

Sunny went weak. Brett just laughed, drank heartily of his champagne, then finished with a kiss that tasted of expensive wine and pleasure. He leaned his forehead against hers and chuckled, whispering against her ear, "Your parents are wonderfully refreshing."

"They have their moments," she conceded, wishing for the briefest of seconds that this was real. But she knew, too soon, the world of nuptials between the Hamiltons and the Robbins would all come crashing down.

"Of course," Doug added, "my old lady and me, we never really believed you needed to have a piece of paper to say you were married."

Sunny's senses skyrocketed to red alert. "Dad..."

"It was okay with me if her mother kept her own name."

Both of the Hamiltons swiveled to look at Sylvia.

"But we did get married," Sylvia said, raising her finger. "A little late, but we did tie the knot."

"That was Sunny's doing," Doug said, nodding. "She insisted on it."

"You never married when—" Lady Miriam flapped her hand "—Sunny was born?"

"Oh, my, no. At the time that would have been one more thing to bother with, wouldn't it?" Sylvia laughed.

Lady Miriam's hand went from flapping to fanning. She looked as if she was going to swoon.

Doug winked at Lord Arthur. "Never bought into the system. That, organized religion, or any of the bureaucracy the government likes to hand out. But our Sunshine? She's as traditional as it comes. She's by the book."

"She was so cute. She just marched in one day—eleven years old—and said that for her own mental health and well-being, she wanted us to get married. Well, what were we going to do?" Sylvia asked. "Sunny planned everything, beginning to end. I always joked that we had our little 'wedding planner' stand up with us."

"Smart girl," Lord Arthur said.

"At least she has some sense," Lady Miriam concurred.

"So when are you two setting the date?" Sylvia pressed.

"Oh, not for a while," Sunny said. "We don't want to rush into anything."

"But you can't wait forever," Brett's mother admonished. "You don't want history to repeat itself."

Sunny blinked, realizing she was referring to the mock pregnancy. Brett's arm circled her shoulders. "There will be more than enough time for everything," he said. "Just give us some time to talk all this over and we'll let you know what we plan to do. We just want to enjoy this minute, this time of having our families together."

The conversation ebbed and flowed, circling around Brett and Sunny. It was polite, it was fun, it was poignant. And all it did was leave Sunny wondering how they were going to talk themselves out of this mess—without any hurt, repercussions or regret.

They were alone in their bedroom, slipping out of their dress clothes. In the living room, Lord Arthur and Lady Hamilton were having a nightcap.

"We have to tell your parents that there is no baby," Sunny implored, turning to Brett. She was in her slip, one that was cut down the middle and up one side. But she figured that wasn't any more—or any less—provocative than her nightgown, the one that she'd worn beside Brett in bed for the last week. "We have to tell them. Before this goes any further. Before they run into my parents in the complex and tell them."

"It's my only real leverage with my parents. They'll be going in a couple of days and—"

"Brett, if my parents think I'm expecting a baby..." She left the rest unsaid. "It's enough for them to think that we're engaged and sleeping together and—"

He vacillated, his amusement vanishing. "I've put you in a compromising position, haven't I?"

"Yes." She slipped on her robe, belting it.

Brett crossed the room and automatically straightened the lapels on her robe. "I'm being selfish. You've been helping me out, and now you've gotten caught in all this. I didn't mean for it to happen."

"I know." Sunny would have carried out any charade, any fantasy, if she could only make this fleeting moment of intimacy last.

"I don't know how I'll tell them." His fingertips slid to her elbows. "I dare say they'll be disappointed. They're already convinced you're carrying the heir to the Hamilton dynasty."

"Brett..." She reached up to trace his cheek, his jaw. "We both know we've taken this too far. Someday you'll find someone to marry, someone to give you a child and make your parents happy. But for now…''

''I know.'' His eyes bored into hers, glowing with a heat she could feel in her bones. ''But for now, you aren't ready to be the mother of my children.''

Taking her by the hand, he led her out into the living room, where his parents relaxed.

''Mother? Father? I have something to tell you.'' Lord Arthur looked up from the paper; Lady Miriam turned the television on mute. ''There's been a misunderstanding. About the baby.''

''The baby? Is everything okay?'' they asked simultaneously.

''It's fine. Well, no, it's not. Fine, I mean. It's just… not.''

Lady Miriam paled and straightened on the sofa. Lord Arthur put his paper down, his face drawn with concern.

''I'm sorry. I shouldn't have told you last week that we were having a baby.'' He squeezed Sunny's fingers and drew her up against him. ''I was so excited at the possibility I wasn't thinking straight. We both want children, but—''

''But what about the baby?'' Lord Arthur said irritably, rising off the chair. ''You are expecting a baby, aren't you?''

''Well, not exactly.''

''That wasn't the truth?''

''I hoped, at the time—well, maybe I wanted there to be one. But—''

Seeing the explanation was going badly, Sunny plunged in, coming to Brett's rescue. ''No, there isn't a baby,'' she said. She didn't want his parents to be disappointed in him. ''Brett thought from something I said that we were having a baby. It's all a terrible mistake.''

''Then you don't *have* to get married,'' Lord Arthur said.

''Oh, no. Not at all. Although I'd dearly love to have a baby with Brett. But not before marriage.'' Offering her most apologetic look, Sunny twisted her hands and delivered the coup d'grâce. "You see, we're only getting married because we love each other. That's the most important reason."

His parents said nothing, but Sunny detected a hint of disappointment in Lady Miriam. Lord Arthur looked as though he needed to reassess the situation.

"Even so, I have to admit I'm terribly disappointed," Brett said, his expression glum. He dropped his chin across the top of Sunny's head and nuzzled her hair as he wrapped his arms around her middle.

She twisted in his embrace to look up at him. "It will be okay," she said softly. "Maybe another time."

"Yeah. Maybe." His voice, strangely husky, sent goose bumps over her flesh. His eyes were too serious, too pensive. She had the oddest feeling he meant what he'd said.

"Children," Lady Miriam finally announced, breaking into the poignant, elusive moment, "your father and I have been talking. We've decided not to go home on Sunday. We'd like to do some sightseeing and extend our visit."

Sunny felt Brett tense. Maybe she'd misread his feelings. Maybe he was ready to move her out, send them home and dispense with the charade. "You're staying?"

"Not here. Your mother wants to travel down the coast, maybe to the Carolinas."

"We'll come back," his mother assured them. "We still have some things we need to discuss, Brett." The statement was clear; he was not yet off the hook about the marriage or the inheritance. "But getting to know Sunny and her family—" his mother looked away, as if groping for the right explanation "—has been an experience, and we realize there's more to know. About the two of you, and your plans."

"We decided to make the most of this visit, son."

"Wonderful. We'd love to have you," Brett said jocularly. "Both Sunny and I are tied up in meetings next week and we do have a company dinner party, so actually it would be a good time for you to have a holiday. But the guest bedroom is always yours. Right, darling?"

"Of course." Sunny said the expected thing, but inside she was aching. She didn't know how much longer she could go on pretending that she cared for Brett. The sad truth was she was beginning to care. Too much.

Once in their bedroom, they each grew quiet. Brett snagged the dangling belt of Sunny's robe and drew her to him. He sank down on the mattress and pulled her into the open V of his legs. "There's absolutely no point in you moving back to the guest room," he said. "I know this isn't how we planned it, but…"

"Yes?"

His palms spanned her waist, his fingers inching over her hips. "It will drive me crazy to move you in and out. It will drive me crazy to think of you sleeping in there, alone. I've gotten used to you keeping the other side of the bed warm."

"Brett, we don't want to mix up this favor I'm doing for you with something else."

"Who's mixing it up?" he grumbled. "I rather like this arrangement, luv. Don't you?"

Her mouth went all watery, and she swallowed, trying to figure out what to say, or how much to reveal. An arrangement? She didn't know if that was what they had, or if that was even what she wanted. One thing was certain: she wanted more of Brett Hamilton. But getting him, keeping him and being in his life was ridiculously complicated. "I like the arrangement," she reluctantly admitted. "But now I have to worry about my parents. Because they think we're engaged, as well."

His thumbs circled the soft part of her belly. "Mmm. Might as well keep your things in my bedroom then. Might as well keep *you* in my bedroom. For they'd expect it if we're living together."

"But it goes against everything I ever said I'd do about love and marriage."

He offered her his boyish, irresistible grin. "But that was before me."

"Definitely before you." She tweaked his ear, then threaded her fingers through his hair, letting them slide to his nape. He felt so good, and she wanted more. He'd grown on her, heightening her senses until she couldn't get enough of him.

"Besides," he argued, "we'd never know when my parents could drop back in. You need to be here, to keep up the charade. And, you know, I think my dad would kind of like another ride in that VW bus."

Sunny groaned. "For a moment there I thought your mother had been hypnotized by that peace symbol dangling from the rearview mirror."

He chuckled. "Yes, she was almost catatonic there for a bit, wasn't she?"

"Brett, why are you doing this to me?" Sunny almost wailed. "I've given you two weeks of my time, and now your life has lapped over into mine. My parents believe we're engaged, your parents thought I was going to have a baby. This is getting too complicated! I was even starting to think I'd begun to show!"

He laughed and patted her tummy. "What do you want first? A boy or a girl?"

"Brett. It isn't a laughing matter. We're getting far too familiar with each other. Like just now. You shouldn't be touching me like this and I..." One of his eyebrows lazily lifted, as if challenging her to admit that she wanted him— and all the sexy little moves he offered. "I didn't intend to get to know you on this kind of a personal level."

His lower lip twitched. "Personal is the next step to intimate."

"Brett!" She feigned outrage and playfully bopped him

on the shoulder. ''I can't continue to sleep in your bedroom!''

He chuckled, the sound rumbling seductively in his chest. ''What's a guy got to do to keep you in his bed?''

Chapter Thirteen

Sunny stayed in his bed—and Brett felt that was the way it should be. He couldn't see any point in playing musical bedrooms, though he did regret that her parents thought they were engaged now, as well. It would be more difficult for her after they broke up, for she'd be living with her parents in the same apartment complex, seeing him at work, and she'd be the one doing the explaining about how things didn't work out. Knowing Sunny, though, she'd make the explanation believable. She'd probably document her decision with a dozen different arguments as to why the relationship wasn't feasible.

The woman was focused and on track. She had an uncanny knack for helping him with his work, and making observations about situations he'd never really noticed before. He trusted her so much he even asked her to read his grandfather's will and tell him what she thought about it.

It was getting too easy to call her on the phone during working hours and say, "Sunny, something's come up. I want your opinion." He caught himself in the staff lounge saying Sunny said this or Sunny said that. Some of the other employees at Wintersoft still looked at him as if they wondered what he and Sunny Robbins had in common.

If only they knew.

If only they knew that her hair smelled like morning rain after she stepped out of the shower. If only they knew that across the breakfast table her smile was a wisp of sunshine. That her laughter was a refreshing breeze, her gentle sigh when she slept a song.

Her parents must have known all those years ago when they named their only daughter that she would reflect sunny climes and have a constant disposition.

Brett liked the way Doug always called her Sunshine, never Sunny.

It fit.

Just as neatly as Sunny was fitting into his life.

He'd intended that, this week when his parents were gone, Sunny and he would head their separate ways. He had some work he could catch up on, and Sunny professed that she wanted time alone. But they couldn't seem to manage it. Neither of them wanted time alone; they wanted time together.

Monday Brett snagged tickets for the New England Patriots. He could have asked Bryan from marketing if he wanted to go—and probably should have—but it didn't seem right. Brett couldn't imagine Sunny sitting home alone, not when they could be bundled up together, a single blanket over their laps as they ate hot dogs and cheered for a first down. So they'd gone to the game together. For hours afterward, Brett had lain awake next to Sunny, who was wearing the Patriots nightshirt he'd gotten her, and wondered how a football game could provide so many incredibly endearing memories.

On Tuesday, they decided to go to a movie. That same day, all the guys in the office had given their pick a thumbs-down, declaring it a don't-waste-your-time chick flick. Still, when the sweet parts brought a tear to Sunny's eye, Brett had gladly handed her his handkerchief, his heart clenching

as he did so. The sexy parts, on the other hand, made him
casually drop his arm around Sunny's shoulders and imagine her in his bed, sharing the most intimate of pleasures.
At that minute, it was her face he'd seen on the screen, her
voice he'd heard.

It was all of her, and it was driving him crazy.

On Wednesday night, he insisted they go to Cheers, the
famed Boston neighborhood bar that had inspired the television show of the same name. In a secluded booth, they'd
grabbed a bite to eat.

He pushed his plate back. "This week's going pretty
well without my folks, isn't it?" he asked.

Dipping another french fry in her ketchup, Sunny pointed
it at him. "Who'd have thought it? I imagined we were
staying together merely for convenience' sake. But..." She
popped the french fry in her mouth.

"Yes?"

"It's getting so I like being around you," she conceded.

He couldn't hide his grin. "Is that bad?"

Tilting her head at a coquettish angle, she said, "It could
be. You are leading me off the straight and narrow. You're
indulging me. You're showing me how to have fun." She
sipped her drink. "I've never been to a football game in
my whole life. My parents don't believe in competitive
sports. But you know, I've never felt such a rush of adren-
aline. I never knew that sitting outside in the cold could
make you feel so warm."

Brett leaned across the table. "It was probably me," he
confided, whispering. "The girls in sales think I'm hot."

He got the intended response: Sunny laughed and a glimmer of pink stained her cheeks. "You are. Outrageously
so."

"Terrific. Then I no longer have to convince you."

"Yes, you do," she retorted. "You have to convince me
by taking me to restaurants like this and movies like last
night. I feel like I'm being paid back for all the trials and
tribulations you've put me through. For *engaging* me."

"We've got another trial to go through tomorrow night," he warned. "That dinner party at Lloyd's house. I wish we could back out."

"What?"

"It's one of our few last days together. Call me anti-social, but I don't want to share you. Not with everybody else. I want you all to myself. We have so much fun together." The words tumbled out before he could call them back, before he could realize the significance of them.

Sunny had butterflies in her stomach when she dressed. She didn't know why this evening upset her. She had spent days with Brett. Nights, too. But this was different. Being escorted to an office function by him was like going on a date.

Brett had easily brushed over the subject with Lloyd, saying that since they lived in the same apartment complex, he might as well bring Sunny. The comment might have stung, but Sunny knew Brett thoroughly enjoyed keeping their relationship a secret.

The problem was it was becoming a harder secret to keep. They kept gravitating toward each other, both at work and in their private lives.

Sunny smoothed a hand over the black sheath and thought about what her mother always said. *Basic black. You can dress it up or dress it down.*

It was also the color for mourning and seduction. Sunny was indeed mourning the fact that her days with Brett were almost over, and seduction, somehow, kept playing at the back of her mind. She couldn't help it. She kept wondering what it would be like to make love to him.

His good-night kisses were pushing the boundaries of good sense and restraint. They left her tingling with aware-ness and want. At the most inopportune moments she thought of how his lips felt on hers: when she was in a think-tank legal meeting; when they passed in the hall; when she caught one of the secretaries flirting with him.

The last was either that or jealousy—and Sunny had been raised without a single jealous bone in her body.

It was vexing, all of it. She wanted to brag that she knew every intimate detail about Brett Hamilton. She wanted to shout that she'd shared his kisses, his laughter, and she wanted to hold his hand in public. She wanted to make a statement that said, "He's mine!" But of course, she couldn't. She couldn't even define their relationship—because she wasn't sure they had one.

It had started as a game, and now all these feelings and emotions had gotten tangled up with it. She and Brett were wearing too many faces, public and private, and Sunny no longer knew which were genuine.

She fingered the pearls at her neck. They gave the classic dress, which was neither low-cut nor too tight, a sultry, sexy appeal. She wondered vaguely if Brett would notice. Grabbing her purse, and refusing to consider the matter further, she walked into the living room.

Brett stood pensively at the fireplace, his elbow resting on the mantel. He turned when she entered, sliding an appreciative gaze from her toes to her dress to the pearls. When his eyes met hers they were smoldering.

"You trying to impress the boss?" he asked huskily. "Word has it that the vice president of the overseas division is a real playboy. You might not be safe, not with him sitting across the table."

"I'll take my chances," Sunny answered.

Brett slowly dropped his arm. "And I keep taking mine. But the crazy thing is, Sunny, I never know if I'm winning or losing. Not with you."

Something twisted in her midsection, making her feel vulnerable and desired. "You've won me over, if that's what you want to know."

"Hah," he muttered to himself. "That's not half of what I want to know." He shook his head as if flinging away some vision, and picked up her coat and walked over to her, opening it so she could slip her arms in the sleeves. "We don't want to be late, or people's tongues may wag."

There, Sunny thought dismally, he'd laid out the parameters once again. They were supposed to be polite and pleasant to each other in public. That and nothing more. The entire thing was becoming a burden—particularly to her wayward heart.

Their drive was unusually silent. While Brett's eyes kept drifting to the gap in her coat, where the hem of her dress inched above her knees, he said little. He seemed distracted, as if something was bothering him.

Finally Sunny said, "Your parents are due back anytime, aren't they?"

"They called while you were getting dressed. They'll be back on Saturday evening. But I don't want to talk about it now." He signaled for the turn onto Lloyd's street.

"Why? Did they say something to upset you?"

"I said I didn't want to talk about it," he said almost irritably, pulling into the first available parking spot, behind Emily's car.

Feeling she had been dismissed, Sunny drew back. "I—"

"No. It's not you," he said quickly. "Or maybe it is. You and this goofy charade we've found ourselves in. But it's too late to change things tonight, so let's just do the British thing. Stiff upper lip and all that. We'll bluster through it."

"If that's what you want," she said softly, regretfully.

This time Sunny didn't wait for Brett to open her car door, but instead met him on the sidewalk. He frowned slightly, as if something was amiss, but offered her his arm. Emily and her date, Marco, an infamous Boston playboy, also stood on the sidewalk in front of the brownstone, waiting for them.

"Hey, you two, you're the last to arrive," she chided. "I was beginning to worry that you'd missed the turn."

"Sorry, no, it just took us—me—" Sunny clarified

quickly, "longer than I expected. You know how, some days, you just run late?"

"Me?" Emily scoffed. "Never. But I've been known to keep my man waiting from time to time." She looped her arm through Marco's and winked up at him as they approached the iron-and-glass front door. A uniformed man held it open and directed them to the lift.

"I wasn't keeping Brett waiting," Sunny protested, "I—"

"Was keeping me in suspense," Brett interjected. "And it was worth it, don't you think, Em?" he asked, nodding to Marco. They had all met at a previous cocktail party.

Emily gave Sunny an assessing look as they entered the marble-lined elevator. "Yes. Definitely. Sunny, I've got to say you seem different lately, and I can't put my finger on it. What's going on with you, anyway?"

"Me? Nothing." She lifted both palms. "I'm just trying out a few new things, like seeing Boston from a tourist's point of view. And Brett got tickets to the Patriots the other night. I'd never been to a football game before."

"Just the two of you went?" Emily asked.

"I only could get a pair," Brett explained.

"You should have joined us, man," Marco said expansively. "My company always gets a box. It's pretty plush, but I can't say that we're always watching the game. You know how it goes, a lot of glad-handing. A few drinks, a few deals."

Brett nodded. "Maybe sometime. Sure."

The elevator opened at the fourth floor, and soon they were entering the foyer of Lloyd's opulent apartment. Jack Devon, Wintersoft's vice president of strategy and business development, stood in the dining room doorway, a flute in hand. He cast an appraising glance at Emily, then Marco. "Brett," he said evenly. "Sunny." Jack, an intensely private man, often showed up with a beautiful woman on his arm. Tonight was no exception. "This is Trish, everyone," he announced, as a lovely brunette floated to his side.

"Trish, meet Emily, Lloyd's daughter, senior vice president of global sales, and her date, Marco Valenti, vice president of sales of Richland Advertising. Sunny Robbins, who is a paralegal at Wintersoft, and Brett Hamilton, who's in charge of the overseas operation. You've already met Lloyd and Carmella."

Trish waved, then turned on a hundred-watt smile. She was all capped teeth and full, sensuous lips. "Nice to meet you all," she said shyly, moving even closer to Jack's side.

Lloyd Winters stepped through the doorway. "Come on, kids," he said. "Don't stand around. We've got a lot of food to eat."

They offered Lloyd their coats and the party moved to the dining room, where an endless buffet of appetizers waited on a side table. The tables were festively adorned with dozens of bright-colored mums, and strewn with ribbon in shades of burnished brass and burgundy.

"Oh, my gosh, Dad!" Emily gushed.

"This is beautiful," Sunny said, brushing her fingertips across the nearest cadmium-colored mum.

"I'm trying out a new catering company for the Christmas party," Lloyd said, waving off the extravagance. "Figured you kids ought to enjoy it, as hard as you all work."

"And try these scallops," Carmella said, as she plucked an appetizer from a tray offered by one of the catering staff. "I can barely keep up with all the good food they're turning out."

Sunny gazed over at Brett, who was strolling toward her with two flutes in his hand. "I've got cabernet for myself, but figured you might like the sparkling grape juice better," he murmured.

She accepted the glass he handed her. "Thank you. But try this." She dipped a cube of bread into the crab dip on her plate and offered it to him. "It's delicious."

Emily leaned in as he greedily ate from Sunny's fingertips. "We have spoons and forks, you know," she teased.

"Sunny, do you usually get Brett to eat right out of your hand?"

She laughed. "No. It takes practice."

After they filled their plates, they gathered in the living room, talking about business, movies and the latest best-sellers. It was a congenial group, but Brett sensed an undercurrent of tension. Marco liked to impress, often bringing the conversation back to his work, his business. Jack appeared annoyed by Marco, but listened indulgently to his stories. And there seemed to be some strange conspiracy between Emily and Carmella, one Brett couldn't quite fathom.

Before dinner, he found himself cornered by Emily. They'd gotten sidetracked discussing a new business deal he'd set up in Portugal, and every one else let them have at it.

"Brett," she said quietly, changing the subject, "what's up with you and Sunny? I know you're living together for your parents' benefit, but you don't have to keep up the pretense here. Or at the office, either."

"Excuse me?"

"You and Sunny," she prompted. "You're getting to be a package deal. I never see one of you without the other."

"Well, I…we—" He broke off, his gaze wandering across the room to seek out Sunny. It was true. They'd somehow become a pair. He couldn't imagine doing anything without her. "We're friends," he explained simply.

"Friends?"

"I like being with her. There's no pretense about that."

But the truth, he silently, ruefully, admitted, was that he didn't just like being with Sunny, he *loved* being with her. And it was destined to be over too soon.

Chapter Fourteen

Brett hadn't been the same since the dinner party at Lloyd's. They'd had a wonderful time, and Sunny hadn't laughed so much in her life. Yet in the twenty-four hours since the party, he'd become distant. Sunny wondered what she'd done.

After work on Friday night, she flopped on the sofa and tucked her feet beneath her to read the newspaper. Only nothing she read made sense, so she put the paper aside. "This could be our last night together," she said. Her voice was low and far more quizzical than she meant it to be.

"Looks like it." Brett loosened the knot on his tie and dumped the stack of unread mail on the desk.

"And soon it will all be over."

"Yeah."

His reply drew her attention. Brett never said "yeah." That was out of character for him. It vaguely occurred to her he that he could be as uncomfortable with their parting as she'd been with their coming together.

"So if there's anything I want to know about you, I have to ask tonight. Or—" she absently ran the tip of her nail over a corner of the newspaper "—if there's any unfinished business between us, we need to address it now."

Brett turned his head to look at her sharply, assessingly. Then he wordlessly moved to the windows, his hands behind his back.

"I'm not going to go all heavy on you, Brett," Sunny said, unconsciously using one of her father's pet phrases. "But I have some unfinished business." He looked over his shoulder at her. "I've always wanted to know if that fireplace works."

Confusion crimped his brow.

"We've never spent a lot of time just hanging out," she explained, rising. She walked to his side and ran her hand over the exquisite mantel. "Can you roast marshmallows in one of these things?"

"I—I don't know."

"Want to find out?"

His rakish, familiar grin slowly spread across his face.

"My mother never let me have marshmallows," she confided. "Too much refined sugar. So we always had all these fires on the beach without any marshmallows—and now, with you, I have the marshmallows without any fire."

The strangest look entered his eyes. "You," he declared finally, "were a deprived child."

"Mmm. But my parents gave me other things instead."

"And I'm glad they did. Because," he said, kneeling in front of the fireplace, "this gives me one more thing I can share with you."

The flames in the gas fire flickered on, and a warm, penetrating heat oozed against Sunny's legs. She took a step back to admire the effect, while Brett rose and touched the switch beside the fireplace to dim the interior lighting.

"That's almost too beautiful," she said approvingly.

"Doug would say something about it being artificial."

"But Sylvia? Now she would say something about not cutting down any trees and not wasting our resources."

''Both of my parents would say a fire requires a glass of sherry, not a bag of marshmallows.''

Brett and Sunny looked at each other and laughed.

Seconds slipped away as their gazes held. The blue-tipped flames lapped hungrily at the faux logs and cast warm shadows about the room. It bathed their features in a soft light, and somehow all the differences between them faded and blurred.

Brett slowly, reluctantly, tore his eyes from her and went to the sofa, where he pulled the chenille throw off the back. He shook it out and spread it on the floor. ''Our blanket,'' he announced unnecessarily. ''I'll see what I can do about a fork for our gourmet tastes.''

Sunny knelt down on the blanket, glad she was wearing a light pair of slacks and a sweater. Behind her, she heard Brett rustling in the kitchen, then the light went out.

''This is the best I can do,'' he said, offering her the long-handled kitchen fork. He held a bag of marshmallows and a dessert plate with one hand as he dropped down beside her.

She took the marshmallows as he pulled his tie free and dropped it onto the carpet beside them. While she ripped open the bag and poked two marshmallows on the tines of the fork, he rolled up his sleeves.

She tried not to watch. The gesture was riveting. Amazingly sexy, amazingly masculine. A funny little tingle started behind her breastbone.

''I think this is an American tradition,'' she said, trying to be offhanded and flip.

''Sometime when you come to England I'll show you real tradition. Real pomp and circumstance.''

She held the marshmallows near the heat. ''Oh, am I invited?''

''Of course.'' He paused, then reached over to place his palm across the back of her hand, and turn the fork, so the marshmallows were on their side. He left his hand there, all warm and thrilling and possessive. "I'd have a grand time showing you about, luv."

Sunny's heart tripped double time. The marshmallows swelled, but she barely noticed.

He pulled the fork back ever so slowly, ever so carefully. He leaned closer to her, until her back and shoulder were against his chest. His chin was next to her ear, and the stubble of his cheek caught her hair. He was so close she could hear every rasping breath he took...and it made her think of the kisses they had shared for everyone's benefit. Everyone's benefit but theirs.

From beneath lowered lashes she gazed up at him. He appeared intent on roasting the marshmallows, but she knew he wasn't; he was intent on her.

"Did I tell you?" she asked, barely able to breathe the words. "Doug found a job on a farm. In Vermont. Like they wanted."

"No!" Brett shifted to look down at her, then abruptly remembered to pull the marshmallows from the fire. He offered the first one to her. She slipped her hand from beneath his to pluck it from the tines.

Admiring it, she continued, "It's the next best thing to owning one for them. Doug never had a real job, so they don't have any savings, but..." She lifted a shoulder and took a tentative bite of the marshmallow. "Ooh, heaven."

He chuckled and tried the other melted marshmallow, licking his fingers after he popped the entire thing in his mouth.

"Do another," she urged, her own mouth full, her sticky fingers fumbling with the plastic bag.

Laughing at her impatience, he put another pair on the tines. "And the rest of the story is...?"

"Oh. They're going to raise goats, and Mom's going to do the soap and candle thing. And..." Sunny hesitated. "I'm getting my apartment back. So by the time your parents leave, you'll be able to have this place all to yourself again."

His gaze flicked to her, going dark and brooding. Just as quickly he turned his attention back to the fireplace. ''And that's the good news.''

''I guess. I'll be out of your way.''

''No. What you're saying is you'll go your way and I'll go mine.''

''Exactly. Just like we both wanted.''

He snorted. ''When we started this game I didn't think I'd want the things I want now.''

A glimmer of hope surfaced in Sunny. ''Such as…?''

He lifted a shoulder. ''I never wanted the marriage and the family stuff. Mostly, I suppose, because my family pushed it so much. But being with you has made me rethink my priorities.''

''They've changed?''

''Let's just say I'm not as skittish about being tied down as I was before. There are times I wake up now and figure I've got one more day ahead of me that looks like an adventure.'' He poked the fork a little farther into the fireplace. ''You once said I was a playboy. Maybe I gave that impression, intentionally. Because I was weary of being under my family's high-profile thumb. Because I didn't want to give any woman I was with the idea I was looking for anything other than a good time. I wasn't in the market for marriage and I wanted everyone to know it.''

Sunny held up her hand, stopping him from saying more. She didn't think she could bear this kind of rejection, so she put it on her own terms. ''If you're trying to warn me that…those times you kissed me, or when we held hands, or you acted all lovey-dovey in front of your parents didn't mean anything, I know that, Brett, and—''

''No. I'm not saying that. I'm saying that deep inside of me, I've always yearned to fall in love. To have a committed, faithful relationship. But…'' He pulled the marshmallows away before they burned. He held them aloft, suspended, as both he and Sunny lost interest in anything but each other. Finally, he dropped the fork and the marshmallows to the plate, forgotten. "Being with you made me realize marriage doesn't have to be a proposition," he said softly. "It can be something I choose. With the woman I choose." He moved to his side to face her, and cupped the back of her neck with his palm.

Sunny shivered as he drew her to him. Her nerve endings throbbed and anticipation flooded her. In the firelight, Brett was a contrast of shadow and light. The angles and planes of his face held an all-male allure, and Sunny desperately wanted to succumb to it.

"So, hey, thank you for giving me that," he said huskily, leaning closer. His breath tickled her lips, and the scent of him made her eyes go heavy with want. He brushed his mouth against hers, as if he were reining himself in, not letting himself go.

In that instant, Sunny realized sadly that Brett Hamilton may have been ready to welcome a woman into his life—but that woman apparently wasn't her.

His parents arrived early on Saturday morning. Brett could tell by the way they moved in that they were on a mission.

"Breton?" his mother asked immediately, glancing down the hall to the master bedroom. "Where is Sunny?"

"She's over at her parents'."

"Oh." His mother's face fell slightly. "Then I guess the situation hasn't changed?"

Brett snorted. "No. If anything, I care more about her now than I ever did."

His father slid his umbrella on the table and rested his hand on the back of the dining room chair. "Sit down, son," he said. "We need to talk. And, honestly, I'd rather do it when Sunny isn't here."

"Why? What did you do, have her family investigated?"

His father arched a brow at him. "That wasn't necessary. They're just people. People with their own value systems, no matter how unconventional."

His mother primly pulled out a chair and sat in it, stiff, erect and no-nonsense. "We've discussed this marriage of yours, Breton," she announced, "at great length. And we've decided not to try and stop you."

A ripple of surprise shot up Brett's spine. "Excuse me?" He looked from his mother to his father. Lord Arthur nodded slowly, as if the gesture pained him. Brett felt his knees give way, and he sank into the opposite chair. His father remained standing.

"She is a good enough woman," he decreed. "Bright, eager, a winning personality. Of course, she is not what we planned for you."

"But then," his mother added starchly, "matters of the heart seldom cooperate with the best laid plans."

"So if you're determined to go ahead with this, and make your life here, with her, on your own, we've decided not to stand in your way. We want you to—" his father cleared his throat "—be happy."

Brett felt as if he'd been hit by a wall of water. He went weak, and his thoughts tumbled a dozen different directions.

"Of course, you'll have to manage this life you've chosen on your own," his father added, "but your mother and I would like to offer to pay for the wedding."

Brett felt frozen. "That's very generous of you, Mother, Father."

"You'll want to have something elegant," his mother said. "Something memorable. Besides, everyone we know in London will want to share in your day, Breton."

"Oh, no, we'd probably just get married here, something simple and—"

"Your father and I want to do this for you, Breton."

"It would mean a lot to us, son, but we do hope you'll choose to marry in London. From what I could tell, Sunny's family doesn't really have ties to any particular area."

Brett debated. They were letting him go! What did it matter where he agreed to get married? It was a moot point, anyway. Then he thought about Sunny and felt inordinately guilty. He imagined her in a white gown, waiting for him at the steps of Winchester cathedral. It would be a fairy-tale wedding. She would be all aglow from the excitement. She would issue that mesmerizing little laugh of hers and knock people out with her down-to-earth goodness. "I'm sure Sunny would be delighted," Brett said softly.

"We need to set the date," his mother said briskly. "Because there's so much to do."

"Call them," his father instructed. "Invite her family to come over and discuss the details. We need to settle this before we return to London."

Brett numbly did as he was asked, figuring it was the best way to get through the charade. When Sunny and her family arrived minutes later, he blurted, "Darling, Mother and Father are pressing us to set the date. So they can begin making plans—because they want to do the wedding for us."

Sunny took a sudden, surprised step backward. Then a slight flush crept up her cheeks. "Oh, I—I haven't thought that far in advance."

"Honey! We're so happy for you!" Sylvia cried, clasping Sunny in a bear hug. Doug hugged them both, then turned to Lord Arthur and extended his hand.

"That's very generous of you, Art. To give my little girl the wedding she's always dreamed of."

"Yes, well, she is marrying my son," he pointed out dryly.

"Sit down," his mother insisted. "I've got a calendar. We'll need to set the date and talk about the ceremony, the reception, the food, the attendants, the colors, the flowers...." She rolled her eyes and shook her head, dramatically adding, "Thank God I'm good at this."

Brett pulled up a chair beside him and patted the seat. "Tell us what you want, Sunny," he invited. "You'll have everything your heart desires. Father's promised to give us a grand wedding."

Sunny slipped into the chair he offered and looked around the table at five sets of expectant eyes. The ultimate irony ate at her: she could have everything she wanted but him. It was all a sham, all of it. Yet she had to see it through.

"Sunny's always been partial to daisies," Sylvia said, gazing fondly at her daughter.

"Yes, well, they're a rather common flower, aren't they?" Lady Miriam replied. "Of course, if we tempered them with yellow roses," she said pensively, "that might do."

"Don't they use a lot of pesticides and fertilizers with hothouse flowers?" Sylvia asked. "Because there's some lovely wildflowers that we could use."

"Mom." The single word held a warning, even though the flowers were an irrelevant issue.

"Let her have what she wants, Syl," her father chided. "She's always wanted a big, fancy wedding."

"You have, dear?" Lady Miriam inquired.

"Well, I—" she shrugged, unable to stop herself from glancing in Brett's direction "—I'd always imagined a white dress, a big church—"

"There's an abbey in Windsor," his mother announced shrewdly, pointing the pen at her husband. "That would be perfect."

"In England?" her parents echoed.

"Well, the church will hold at least a thousand, maybe more."

Sylvia and Doug looked at each other. "We were thinking something like that nice little chapel over in Cambridge, Massachusetts, and the banquet room in the basement. They'd probably do up a nice buffet or something," he offered.

"Buffet?" Lady Miriam looked aghast, then composed herself. "No, waiters with trays of canapés, I think. And a sit-down dinner. Quail would do." She tapped the pen against the calendar. "After all, we did the same for Breton's brother, Phillip."

"Well," Sylvia conceded, squirming on the chair, "maybe we could have a nice little reception here, after the wedding."

"Good thought," Doug murmured. "Cake and punch. A few nuts. I can pay for that."

"Settled," Lady Miriam announced, as if she'd struck a gavel on the table. "Now for the attendants. I'm sure the abbey would accommodate up to eight, maybe ten. On each side."

Sunny felt her jaw sag. Brett gave her a squeeze, making her mouth snap shut.

"Darling?" he inquired.

"I—I haven't thought about it yet."

"Well, Sunny, dear, what would you like?" Lady Miriam asked. "This is, after all, your wedding. You should have some say in the plans."

Sunny, on the spot, didn't have any idea what she should say. She was reluctant to share any of her longings with them—because none of it would ever come to fruition. Her dreams about Brett were just that. Dreams. Unfulfilled. Unrequited.

She hesitated, then looked up at him, aware that he would make the world's most handsome groom, the world's most wonderful husband. It would be so easy to love him, and so impossible not to. He was hers, if only for this fleeting space of time. She would share one little thing…because the rest would all soon be forgotten.

"I've always wanted to be escorted to the church in a horse-drawn carriage," she revealed carefully. "I know that's frivolous, but I'd really, really like that."

"Done," his mother announced, writing frantically in her planner.

Chapter Fifteen

The date was set for June 28. Sunny didn't think she'd ever look at that date again and not have regrets. As it was, she could barely face her parents. They were so excited for her it was shameful. They talked about their daughter doing her own thing, marrying her own English lord. They talked about her getting married in England, with all the trimmings, in a dress with a ten-foot-long train and a footman and a carriage. The illusion was mind-boggling.

Mostly because there was a big hole in the picture. That hole being Brett.

She had fallen hopelessly, helplessly, unequivocally in love with him. And he didn't have a clue! How could he have done this to her? The premise was ridiculous. They'd had a nice little deal going: he'd give her free room and board, she'd give him a fiancée. Falling in love was not part of the bargain—and she knew it.

His parents had left that very afternoon, his mother carrying a notebook full of ideas for the wedding and reception. She assured Sunny she would work on it on the plane. Sunny thanked her, and felt like a fraud.

She was moving out. Now. Before Brett and his cocka-mamie scheme drove her insane. With desire. With longing. With love.

"What are you doing?" Brett demanded. He stood in the doorway of their bedroom, his eyes fixed on the clothes she'd tossed in the suitcase.

"I'm getting out of your way. It's time for me to give you your life back, like you want."

"What? You can't leave now."

"And why not?" She yanked the gorgeous cranberry suit off the hanger and dumped it in the suitcase on top of everything else. "I've done my job. Your parents are convinced there will be a wedding. They are convinced we are happy and content, and—"

"Well? Aren't we?"

Sunny's arms fell limply to her sides. The blouse she held dropped from her hands and puddled on the bed. "Brett, it doesn't matter anymore. It was a great time, but—"

"Yes?"

She stared at him. *But I fell in love with you.* She couldn't very well say that, could she? "But...you taught me how to have fun," she said softly, unexpectedly, her heart nearly breaking as she uttered the words. "I think maybe I need some time to figure out how to do that by myself. I've always been so focused, so determined to keep Sylvia and Doug out of trouble. They were always off doing these wild and crazy things, and there I was, wanting this normal, formal upbringing." She paused, sorely aware of how different their lives were. "And you had it. You had it all, and yet craved the freedom my parents offered me. You didn't take anything seriously, and you had a grand time poking holes in your parents' expectations, their value system, their—"

"A *grand time?*" he echoed. "You're beginning to talk like me. It looks as if a little bit of me is rubbing off on you."

"More than you want to know," she muttered, tossing the blouse in the suitcase.

She reached for the lid, to slam it shut. But Brett's hand settled over hers, stopping her. "Maybe the truth, for both of us, lies somewhere in the middle," he said quietly.

"Maybe," she answered, trying to force indifference into her voice. But her heart was anything but indifferent. She felt too much.

His hand slipped away. "What are you going to tell your parents?"

A dozen thoughts went through her head, most of them lies. It was the truth that surfaced, and nagged at her. "Probably," she said slowly, thoughtfully, "that the temptation of living with you is too great."

His icy-blue gaze went hard.

It occurred to her then that the truth just might set her free, for he'd be able to pursue "the woman of his choice."

"Sunny—"

"Don't," she said too quickly, turning to face him, unconsciously laying a hand on his chest. She felt his heartbeat and realized it ruled her, every integral part of her. Her thoughts, her emotions, her needs, her desires. She wanted him, all of him, and yet he'd never give himself away, not that easily. "It's going to be hard enough to see you at work and be reminded of all this history we share. I'm going to think of that goofy way you arrange your pillow before you go to sleep. Or the way you always put on a sock and a shoe, and a sock and a shoe when you get dressed. Instead of two socks, two shoes—the normal, rational, reasonable way. So how am I going to find legal files, when you walk in the room and I wind up thinking about your socks?"

"Sorry. I believe I've upended your thinking."

"You have," she muttered. "I don't even care about working late anymore! Now I want to check out the newest restaurant, or see a movie, or...or...make candles! My mother asked me if I wanted to make candles with her this weekend, for the wedding, and I said yes! And I even thought it would be *fun*.''

"My. You really have tumbled from the straight and narrow, haven't you?'' His lips twitched. "What kind of candles?''

"Wildflower.''

"American wildflower or English wildflower?''

"I—I don't know. But it doesn't make a difference, anyway. I'm telling her tonight that I've had second thoughts and we're postponing the wedding.''

"You'd do that?''

"Well, I'm going to have to tell her sometime.''

"It's going to be quite a shock for them. They were so excited about you getting married.''

"I'll let them down slowly. But I'll make sure they overhear me cancel the reservations for the chapel in Cambridge.''

His palms slid beneath her elbows, then shimmied up her arms. "Why? Why would you want to do that?'' he asked.

"Because if we let them know early, we'll get all our deposit money back. Your parents' deposit money back,'' she revised.

"I think they'd rather spend it on a wedding.''

"Brett—''

"I've found the woman I love,'' he hinted softly. "It makes sense to keep all the arrangements intact and make it official.''

Sunny's features held a myriad of conflicting emotion. "You...you found someone?''

He chuckled. His hand strayed to hers, to lift her hand and examine her ring finger. "I see you're still wearing the ring.''

"I'll leave it on the dresser.''

"You need to leave it on your finger. And we need to go to work tomorrow morning and make the announcement there. That's where everything first started. It seems appropriate, doesn't it?''

Sunny went weak, so weak she thought her knees were going to buckle. Her heart raced and her thoughts were mush.

"I love you, Sunshine," he said. "I want to marry you, and have that happily ever after story we both grew up reading about. The one where the English lord sweeps the fair damsel off her feet and retires to the English countryside, to make love, trim the roses and raise children."

"You aren't serious, are you?" she breathed, unable to take it all in.

"Not about the English countryside, or the roses part. The countryside is boring and the roses have thorns. No, I'm only talking about the making love and making babies part." He laughed and nuzzled her temple. He bent his head to her and possessively captured her mouth, parting her lips for a deep, passionate kiss. Desire rushed through her, blotting out all her cognitive powers, atrophying her physical strength. He kissed her until she was weak and breathless and incapable of refusing him. Then he reluctantly pulled away. "No, luv, we have too much to do to simply sit back and watch each other grow old. We have a lot of life to live. And since there won't be an inheritance to retire on, I think we should plan on enjoying our jobs at Wintersoft for the next, oh, twenty years or so."

"That sounds like a plan," she said softly, awash in the colors of love, of happiness and hope. Then the realization hit her, and she looked at him in surprise and grasped his shirtfront. "But Brett? Wait. About that inheritance? I have something to tell you."

Brett and Sunny stretched out on the bed, and between kisses, planned their life together. Her clothes, the ones she'd intended to pack, were tangled at their feet. With her head resting on his outstretched arm, Sunny stared at the ceiling.

"I couldn't believe it when I looked at that will you gave me," she said. "I think your grandfather intentionally put that loophole in it. He probably knew that you'd do something like this.''

Brett chuckled and pulled her closer to his side. ''Astute of you to find it. Most likely I would have shrugged it off and forgotten about it, and no one would have known.''

''The only reason I looked at it was because I didn't think it was fair to deprive you of your birthright.'' When he glanced down at her, she added, ''I'm not talking about the title, okay? I just think that you should be able to marry the woman you love—''

''I am.''

Sunny flushed with happiness. ''Without giving up your inheritance,'' she finished.

''It isn't the money, so much. I think it's a pride thing. There is something humiliating about being cut off.'' He lifted his wrist and checked his watch. ''Let's call my parents now. They should be home.''

Sunny raised her head, frowning. ''You're going to tell them about the inheritance?''

''Heavens, no. That would just upset them. And it's not important, anyway. I want to tell them we can't wait any longer and we're moving up the wedding date. No sense in Mother going to all that work for nothing.''

Sunny let her head drop back to his shoulder, and chuckled while he dialed the number one-handed. ''You really are a thoughtful son,'' she said softly.

He grinned down at her and put the phone to his ear. ''Father? Yes, it's me. Brett.'' He paused. ''Put Mother on the other line, will you?''

Sunny turned and wedged an elbow beneath her so she could hear parts of the conversation. She heard rustling and knew that her future in-laws were hurrying to their stations.

''Yes, Brett, I'm here,'' Lady Miriam said.

''Mother, Father, Sunny and I have been talking this over. We don't want to wait until the end of June to get married. We *can't* wait that long. I mean, Sunny has all these old-fashioned ideas about—well...''

On the other end of the line both his father and mother burst out laughing. Sunny cringed.

"You're living together, so it's a little late to be old-fashioned, son," his father advised him. "And as for the wedding, we talked of little else."

"The entire way home," his mother stated.

"We've been thinking this over, Brett—and we've changed our minds." The pause over the lines was positively pregnant. Both Sunny and Brett stared at the phone with wide eyes. "We've never seen you so happy, Brett. It's obvious to us Sunny belongs in your life. We want you to know we approve."

"Whenever you want to get married is fine, Brett. Let us know the date you choose, and I'll take care of things at this end," his mother offered. "Of course, I'd like to offer you a memorable affair, and all your friends will want to meet your new bride."

"I want them to, Mother. I can't wait to introduce Sunny to everyone." His fingers slipped into her hair, threading through the glossy strands.

"And your father has something else to tell you, dear."

Lord Arthur cleared his throat. "About that inheritance, son...you've made your own way into a productive life, and you've found yourself a lovely wife. How can I fault you for doing all the right things? I don't think it would be right to take anything away from you. I told your mother last night that I want to see you get your inheritance—and she agrees. You need everything you can get to start out well in life these days. And I'd never think that you were taking advantage of it, just because you were born to it."

"This—this change surprises me, Father."

"You've earned it," Lord Arthur said gruffly. "Every bit."

"Thank you. I—"

"You don't need to thank me for what's rightfully yours. Now you just go and have a happy life with that bride of yours."

"We love you, Brett," his mother said. "Say hello to Sunny for us."

"Oh, and Brett?" his father went on jovially. "Your brother's here. I think he wants to talk to you."

"Phillip?"

"Brett, old boy, I've got news." The excitement in his brother's voice was palpable. "The doctor was wrong! Last night Carolyn went into labor, and we have a boy! Three girls and a boy!"

"Well, congratulations, you cagey old bloke, you!" Phillip laughed. "You mean I'm off the hook? About offering up an heir and getting married?"

"It does appear so, yes."

Brett chuckled, realizing the plot behind his "arranged" engagement would have to remain a secret. At least for a while. "I'm getting married, anyway. It's something you've got to do when you find the perfect woman."

Their goodbyes were poignant. By the time Brett depressed the Talk button, Sunny's eyes were red-rimmed and she was blinking furiously. "You okay?" he asked.

She nodded. "That was so sweet. Your mother and father really are softies, aren't they? And they let your brother tell you about the new baby."

"Ah, yes. Beneath that starchy British facade a few hearts do beat," he teased. "I want you to know, Sunny, we don't need to worry about heirs—and we are independently wealthy." Her eyes grew round. "But with that comes a responsibility." She nodded, taken in by his seriousness. "You have to choose charities, you have to share." She wordlessly nodded again. "I still want to work for Wintersoft. But I've had this idea for some time now...."

"What?"

"Jake, in accounting, uses this American expression—'Bought the farm,' or something like that."

"It means the end of things."

"Not anymore. It means the beginning of things. A

whole new farm, a whole new life." Sunny's eyes narrowed as she wondered what he meant. "I want to buy a farm in Vermont for your parents, Sunny. They should have that. They should own it instead of working on it. Then we'd know they were settled and could ease into retirement. Your dad can raise zucchinis and tap maple trees. He can have all the pancakes and syrup he wants. Your mother can make candles and soap. They're good people, and they do make a contribution to life." He grinned. "Particularly to yours."

"Oh, Brett...I can't believe..." She shook her head, her eyes fluttering closed.

"And it would be one less worry for you," he said.

"But—"

"And it would make a wonderful place for their grandchildren to play."

Her heart tripped in her chest. "Have I told you how much I love you, Brett Hamilton?"

"Not nearly enough, luv, not nearly enough."

Epilogue

Emily and Carmella arranged the plates, napkins and plastic utensils on the tables in the main conference room for an early morning meeting at Wintersoft. Lloyd always insisted that if his employees came to work early, they deserved a breakfast of coffee, pastries and fruit.

"Can we help you do something?" Sunny Robbins offered. Brett, as was his habit of late, stood attentively at her side.

"I think we're all set," Carmella said, standing back to look over the table. "So what's up with you two? You're here early."

Sunny and Brett glanced at each other and smiled. Sunny nervously twisted a ring on her finger, then offered it up for their inspection. "We're getting married," she announced. "We wanted you to be the first to know."

"What?" Emily made a dive for the ring, to turn it beneath the fluorescent lights. "Carmella, look!"

Brett grinned, as both Carmella and Emily exclaimed over the setting. "Actually, I already told Lloyd. I told him that Sunny and I may be working a lot more closely in the future. Behind closed doors, and on a private liaison.''

"Congratulations," Emily offered, laughing, as she gave Sunny a hug. "This office is becoming a real hotbed of romantic activity. We had a lot of bachelors around here, they're dwindling fast.''

"Best wishes," Carmella agreed. "I'm so happy for you both.''

Later, after the couple moved away, Carmella sidled a look at Emily. "Do you realize," she said, "that we have had a fifty percent turnover in our bachelor inventory?''

"I know." Emily's reply was almost gleeful. "Reed, Nate and Jack are the only ones left. And then I'm home free.''

"Maybe not," Carmella warned. "Nate doesn't look at much past his computer screen. And Jack...''

"Jack drives me nuts," Emily admitted. "I can't find out a thing on him, and I can't even begin to imagine who would marry him.''

"All Lloyd will tell me about him is that he's a self-made man and came from nothing. Those are the trickiest kind," she confided, taking the sugar packets out of the box and dumping them in a bowl.

"Reed Connor, on the other hand, may be someone we can marry off. He has a high school sweetheart he's never gotten over.

Emily stopped. "He does? Really?''

"Mmm-hmm," she murmured, winking at Emily. "Everyone has one old unforgotten flame from their past." She offered the box to Emily. "Here, honey. Take these back to the kitchen, will you?''

Emily, nearly giddy to think that she had put one more notch on the bachelor bedpost, took the box and ducked behind her father and Jack, who stood in the doorway of the adjacent kitchen.

"I'm surprised a spoiled rich girl like her can't find a good man," Emily overheard Jack say in a sarcastic tone.

"Rich doesn't mean a thing," her father replied dryly. "No one was more shocked than I was when Todd and Emily's marriage didn't work out. I thought they had it all."

If it was physically possible, Emily's blood pressure would have shot right out the top of her head. They were talking about *her!* She was so incensed she tossed the box of sugar packets into the cupboard and watched them scatter. She most certainly was *not* a spoiled little rich girl! Who did Jack think he was, saying something like that to her father? To her own father?

And for that matter, she didn't need a man to make her happy or to make her life whole, either! When would her father realize that?

"Now a man like you, a man who's pulled himself up from his bootstraps, maybe that's the difference. Maybe I made it too easy for Todd." Her father audibly sighed. "Ah, well. If I can't do anything about my daughter's situation, at least there's enough romance for everyone else in this company."

"Look," Jack said dryly. "The secretarial pool just retreated to the corner to cry their eyes out that Brett Hamilton's been taken out of circulation."

Lloyd laughed. "The thing is, Sunny's such a nice girl that no one will hold it against her for having the winning ticket."

Lloyd moved into the conference room, and everyone grew quiet. "We intended to have a very dry, very dull meeting about sales projections for December," he said. "But as most of you know, we've been overshadowed by a merger—between the overseas division and the legal office." Everyone laughed, and all eyes turned expectantly to Brett and Sunny. In response Brett twined his fingers through hers and raised her hand as if he'd just landed a million-dollar deal.

"I'd like to propose an orange juice toast," Lloyd said. "To Brett and Sunny. Congratulations on your engagement. May you live a long and happy life together, at home and at Wintersoft.''

After they joined in the toast, Brett set their glasses aside. ''We're planning the wedding as quickly as we can,'' he advised the onlookers.

''And you're all invited,'' Sunny added, before he gathered her up in his arms.

She was, Brett realized, going to be a beautiful bride. He felt incredibly lucky. As if he had the best of both worlds. And he did have that! Exactly that.

Why, she'd grown up and thrived on a laid-back lifestyle, an all-natural diet and total commitment to sociological and environmental issues. He, on the other hand, had come from a rigid upbringing of impeccable manners, gourmet tastes and capitalist endeavors. Yet they met halfway and made each other whole.

Sunny, blushing prettily, leaned toward him for a lingering kiss. He took his time and indulged her. ''I love you,'' he finally whispered against her ear, breaking away.

''Forever,'' she offered, the word muffled against the hollow of his neck.

Brett chuckled in satisfaction and lifted her hand to the onlookers. ''And one more thing, just so you'll all share in my surprise for Sunny,'' he said aloud, ''this morning I made arrangements for our honeymoon—at a castle in Scotland.''

He heard Sunny catch her breath as a murmur went through the crowd.

''I want that happily ever after, Sunny,'' he said softly, privately, ''with you. We deserve a fairy-tale beginning. Lord Breton and his unpredictable, irresistible American wife, Sunny. Now—and forever—happily, blissfully, in love.''

*   *   *   *   *

Turn the page for a sneak preview of the next
MARRYING THE BOSS'S DAUGHTER
title featuring Reed and Samantha's
second-chance romance:

SANTA BROUGHT A SON

by Melissa McClone
on sale December 2003 (RS1698)

Chapter One

Don't think about her. Don't think about the past. Don't think about anything except the reason you are here.

"Okay, goodbye, Reed." She stared past him as if he were invisible. Funny, but that's how he'd felt in high school around everyone but her. "Have a safe trip back to Boston. And have a wonderful life, too."

The temperature had dropped more than a few degrees, and he couldn't blame it all on the weather. She might as well have slammed the door in his face.

"Feel better?" Samantha asked.

Reed felt the same way he had the last time he saw her. All tied up in knots and wondering what the future held without her in his life. But this time Art wasn't standing in his way. No one was. And if Reed truly wanted her, he was man enough to get her this time around. "No."

She fiddled with the door lock. "What more do you want?"

He wanted to leave. He had to return to Boston, to his job. He had no time for a long-distance relationship, let alone an affair. But something held him in his place.

Why wasn't closure enough, now that he had it? Because "goodbye" didn't resolve what they had shared so long ago. She had been his first love, his first lover. And last night's kiss had awakened both dormant feelings and memories. Good ones and bad. He realized this wasn't about saying goodbye. Not at all.

Plump snowflakes fell from the sky, landing on the sidewalk and on him. "Sam…"

"It's Samantha."

"Samantha," he repeated. "What happened between us—"

"Was years ago," she interrupted. "Forget about it."

Logically he knew she was correct, but Reed wanted her to admit she'd made a mistake choosing Art over him. And Reed didn't want to leave until he got that. But the longer he stood there, the better he understood it wasn't going to happen.

Snow fell harder. The darkening sky told him this wasn't a passing flurry, though the weather forecast hadn't called for snow. "Would you mind if I came inside and called the airline about my flight?"

She looked into the shop again. "This isn't a good time."

"It'll only take a minute."

With a hint of annoyance in her eyes, she stepped back and opened the door. "Okay."

It wasn't the warmest invitation he'd ever received, but he brushed the snow off himself and stepped inside. "Thanks."

Her store overflowed with holiday cheer. A contrast to the reception he'd received from its owner. The scent of vanilla, cinnamon and pine reminded him of his grandmother's house. White twinkling lights entwined in garland added a touch of whimsy. Stockings of different shapes and sizes were hung on the walls. Ornaments decorated several Christmas trees. Icicles and snowflakes dangled from the ceiling. Menorahs and dreidels filled an entire display rack. Only Christmas carols were missing.

A red Santa hat lay on a table, and Reed placed it on his head. "Ho-ho-ho." He expected a smile. He didn't get one. "Nice shop. Very Christmasy."

"The phone is on the counter by the cash register."

"I have my cellphone," Reed admitted. He called the airline. His flight was delayed. If the snow continued to fall, it would be canceled.

A scream tore through the silence. A blur of blue raced from the back into the store toppling a three-foot-tall Father Christmas figurine. Samantha's quick reflexes kept it from hitting the floor.

A boy wearing a blue sweatshirt and jeans held up a Game Boy. Brown hair stuck out from his baseball cap. "Look. I made it to level six, Mom."

Mom? It shouldn't matter that she'd had a child with another man—her husband—but still Reed's heart tightened. He'd thought of her having kids, but in a detached first-comes-marriage-then-comes-baby sort of way, but seeing it was different. And affected him more than he could have imagined.

He did a double take. The kid looked too old to be hers. Guess she and Art hadn't waited to start a family.

She smiled, though her face had lost some of its color. "That's great, honey."

The tenderness in her voice took Reed by surprise. She sounded like a mom. When he was younger, he'd imagined her as a girlfriend, lover, wife, but never a mother. Of course, he'd been twenty the last time he saw her, and children hadn't been on the edge of his radar screen. The same way they weren't now.

"I didn't have to use the clues from the magazine." The boy bounced from foot to foot. "I did it all on my own."

"You'll have to teach me," she said.

Samantha eyed Reed. Her piercing gaze seemed to be searching for something. What, he didn't know.

"Okay." The boy grinned and a dimple appeared on his left cheek.

Reed touched the spot of his own dimple. Same left side.

The boy looked up at him and his smile widened. "I like your hat."

Reed had forgotten he was wearing it. "Thanks."

"My dad used to wear a Santa hat every Christmas," he said.

"Timmy, this is Mr. Connors." Samantha sounded hoarse, and she cleared her throat. "Reed, this is Timmy. Mr. Connors went to high school with me and your dad," she emphasized the last word. All of her features seemed tight. The wariness Reed had glimpsed last night was back.

"I want to be a pitcher like my dad." As Timmy drew his brows together, two lines formed about his nose. Just like Samantha used to do when she was concerned about an upcoming test or homework assignment. "But I need to learn to throw a curveball first. Do you know how?"

"Playing catch is more my style," Reed admitted. "I never could throw a curveball myself."

"That's okay," Timmy said. "Playing catch is fun, too. I want a new mitt for my birthday."

"When's your birthday?" Reed asked.

"In twelve days. I'll be eight." Timmy smiled. "I'm having my birthday party at the ice rink after school. We're going to skate, play hockey and eat lots of cake."

"Sounds fun."

But eight? Samantha must have gotten pregnant right after graduation. Reed subtracted nine months from Timmy's birthday. The date fell right around spring break. The spring break when they'd made love. Reed glanced at Timmy, at his brown hair and eyes. Art and Samantha had been Fernville High's blond-haired, blue-eyed golden couple. Reed's pulse quickened.

Theoretically he *could* be Timmy's father, but that wasn't possible. They'd used protection. Besides, she would have told him if he were going to be a father. No woman in her right mind would keep a child a secret. No, Timmy wasn't his.

"Want to come to my party?" Timmy asked.

Samantha almost dropped a glass Santa ornament she was hanging on a tree. "Mr. Connors was just leaving for the airport to catch his flight home." Her voice contained a faint tremor, and she lowered her gaze. "We shouldn't keep him any longer."

"My flight's been delayed."

She straightened. "You didn't tell me that."

"You didn't ask."

Timmy studied the screen on his Game Boy. His lips were parted and his tongue was flipped over with the tip showing between his teeth. Reed's heart slammed against his chest. That was the exact thing he did when he concentrated.

It was more than a telling gesture. Timmy looked just like…

Me.

A million thoughts ran through Reed's head, but he kept coming back to one. He might have idealized her in the past, but the Samantha he'd known and loved would never keep the existence of a child—his child—from him. There had to be another explanation.

"It was nice of you to stop by, Reed." Her tone was more resigned than courteous. She moved out of the aisle to clear the way to the door. "But I'm sure you have other places you need to visit before you leave for the airport."

Reed tried to see the resemblance between him and Timmy. Tried and failed. A dimple and brown hair and eyes. Three physical traits. Not solid enough proof. Maybe Reed's mind was playing tricks on him. But that shared gesture… "Not really."

"You could come over to our house," Timmy said. "We're going to decorate our Christmas tree today. It's going to be a lot of fun. And my mom bakes cookies."

As Samantha wet her lips, her jaw tensed. "Don't forget, Mr. Connors's flight has only been delayed, not canceled."

''With this snow, it'll be canceled.'' Fernville was the last place Reed expected to be for another day, but too many questions remained for him to grab his bag and hop on an airplane. ''I'd love to help decorate your Christmas tree. I haven't done that in years.''

She touched Timmy's shoulders and pulled him closer to her. ''If the snow stops—''

''I'll catch a later flight.'' Reed sounded carefree, but that was the last thing he felt inside. He'd learned to control his emotions. Business required it, but it made life easier, too. One more thing he had to thank Samantha Brown Wilson for. What else, Reed wondered, was he going to learn from her while he was here?

* * * * *

✂

Your opinion is important to us! Please take a few moments to share your thoughts with us about your experiences with Harlequin and Silhouette books. Your comments will be very useful in ensuring that we deliver books you love to read. *Please take a few minutes to complete the questionnaire, then send it to us at the address below.*

Send your completed questionnaires to:
Harlequin/Silhouette Reader Survey, P.O. Box 9046, Buffalo, NY 14269-9046

1. As you may know, there are many different lines under the Harlequin and Silhouette brands. Each of the lines is listed below. Please check the box that most represents your reading habit for each line.

Line	Currently read this line	Do not read this line	Not sure if I read this line
Harlequin American Romance	❑	❑	❑
Harlequin Duets	❑	❑	❑
Harlequin Romance	❑	❑	❑
Harlequin Historicals	❑	❑	❑
Harlequin Superromance	❑	❑	❑
Harlequin Intrigue	❑	❑	❑
Harlequin Presents	❑	❑	❑
Harlequin Temptation	❑	❑	❑
Harlequin Blaze	❑	❑	❑
Silhouette Special Edition	❑	❑	❑
Silhouette Romance	❑	❑	❑
Silhouette Intimate Moments	❑	❑	❑
Silhouette Desire	❑	❑	❑

2. Which of the following best describes why you bought *this book?* One answer only, please.

the picture on the cover	❑	the title	❑
the author	❑	the line is one I read often	❑
part of a miniseries	❑	saw an ad in another book	❑
saw an ad in a magazine/newsletter	❑	a friend told me about it	❑
I borrowed/was given this book	❑	other: _____	❑

3. Where did you buy *this book?* One answer only, please.

at Barnes & Noble	❑	at a grocery store	❑
at Waldenbooks	❑	at a drugstore	❑
at Borders	❑	on eHarlequin.com Web site	❑
at another bookstore	❑	from another Web site	❑
at Wal-Mart	❑	Harlequin/Silhouette Reader	❑
at Target	❑	Service/through the mail	
at Kmart	❑	used books from anywhere	❑
at another department store or mass merchandiser	❑	I borrowed/was given this book	❑

4. On average, how many Harlequin and Silhouette books do you buy at one time?

I buy _____ books at one time	❑
I rarely buy a book	❑

MRQ403SR-1A

5. How many times per month do you shop for any *Harlequin and/or Silhouette* books?
One answer only, please.

1 or more times a week	❑	a few times per year	❑
1 to 3 times per month	❑	less often than once a year	❑
1 to 2 times every 3 months	❑	never	❑

6. When you think of your ideal heroine, which *one* statement describes her the best?
One answer only, please.

She's a woman who is strong-willed	❑	She's a desirable woman	❑
She's a woman who is needed by others	❑	She's a powerful woman	❑
She's a woman who is taken care of	❑	She's a passionate woman	❑
She's an adventurous woman	❑	She's a sensitive woman	❑

7. The following statements describe types or genres of books that you may be
interested in reading. Pick *up to 2 types* of books that you are most interested in.

I like to read about truly romantic relationships ❑
I like to read stories that are sexy romances ❑
I like to read romantic comedies ❑
I like to read a romantic mystery/suspense ❑
I like to read about romantic adventures ❑
I like to read romance stories that involve family ❑
I like to read about a romance in times or places that I have never seen ❑
Other: _____ ❑

*The following questions help us to group your answers with those readers who are
similar to you. Your answers will remain confidential.*

8. Please record your year of birth below.

19 ____

9. What is your marital status?

single ❑   married ❑   common-law ❑   widowed ❑
divorced/separated ❑

10. Do you have children 18 years of age or younger currently living at home?

yes ❑   no ❑

11. Which of the following best describes your employment status?

employed full-time or part-time ❑   homemaker ❑   student ❑
retired ❑   unemployed ❑

12. Do you have access to the Internet from either home or work?

yes ❑   no ❑

13. Have you ever visited eHarlequin.com?

yes ❑   no ❑

14. What state do you live in?

_____

15. Are you a member of Harlequin/Silhouette Reader Service?

yes ❑   Account # _____   no ❑   MRQ403SR-1B